The Dancing Plague

A COLLECTION OF UTTER SPECULATION

Edited by

LCW Allingham

River Eno and Susan Tulio

ISBN: 979-8-9868879-0-6

Published by Speculation Publications

DEDICATION

To Patricia, with love and gratitude for her steadfast support and beautiful visions.

CONTENTS

FOREWORD

What is it about the dancing plague that speaks to people? At the edges of the dark ages, amongst populations decimated by the Black Death, by extreme poverty, by the horrors of daily life, people succumbed to something that seems so bizarre to us in the modern age.

And yet so familiar.

Why do musicians, artists, writers and dancers still study it? Still use it as inspiration to create? I think they understand something about it.

I think we all do, if we really admit it.

Listen and let go.

Although the stories of this book are very different from one another, they all hint at some tug within the human soul to release our mortal burdens. To turn to the sky and let our bodies move with a current we cannot see, but we always feel.

There seems to be an understanding deep in the human psyche that a wild energy awaits us, to sweep us away from our grief, our toils, away from our own relentless thoughts and just move us along with the winds.

"Other People's Tsunamis" grabs at something in your soul, the longing and acceptance of an outsider, the difference in how one sees the world is what can ultimately save it.

"This Way Lies Madness" unfolds a story of such fragile beauty that at times it feels like holding butterfly wings, knowing anything but perfect balance means disaster.

"The Consequences of Sin" is sharp, seeming to start out with a laugh, but slowly revealing itself to be a scathing condemnation of the world.

In "The Holy Harvest" the plague is explained innocently by a young girl, who's in a dangerous situation she doesn't quite understand.

The distance between sin and salvation is but a hair's width in "The Third Ministration" as the reader follows a young doctor down a dark path of madness and love.

In "The Spider Whisperer: A Tale of Plague Dances, Peacock Spiders and Pumpkins" a young woman's world expands into legend, through coincidence or maybe fate.

"Interdisciplinary" exposes the consequences of letting egos rule when a tenured professor gets a once in a lifetime opportunity and watches it turn to ash.

The longing of community, acceptance and release of one's grief to music and dance is beautifully illustrated in "Searching for the Perfect Beat."

And lastly, in "Shake, Rattle and Roll" a familiar band of miscreants cause their own brand of chaos in the city of Strasbourg, with the help of a young lady looking for a freer life.

Each story offers a key to this centuries-old mystery. Each one warns us that it could happen again, if we just relinquish control.

I think we all know, somewhere deep down, that it's waiting.

Listen and let go.

I wonder how many of us are tempted.

-LCW Allingham, 2022

Hendrik Hondius (Dutch, 1573–1650). *The Dancing Mania*, 1642. Engraving after Pieter Bruegel the Elder (Dutch, c. 1525/30–1569). Wellcome Collection, London.

Other People's Tsunamis

Jennifer Lee Rossman

There are two kinds of people in this world: those who do magic, and those who are magic.

Most people fall into the first category and don't even know it, laughing away coincidences and conveniently forgetting those little psychic moments because subconsciously, having that kind of power makes people uncomfortable.

But it's real, whether we acknowledge it or not. It's real, it's in us, in everything we do and every motion we make.

We are all butterflies flapping our wings and causing tsunamis.

That's the way it is, the way the world is supposed to work. All of the little butterflies obliviously helping the timeline unfold with their spells disguised as superstitions, rituals disguised as dances. A beautiful order derived from chaos.

Until someone from the second group, someone with too much power and the knowledge to wield it for their own purposes—someone like me, someone like…him—turns order back to chaos. When someone changes things without regard for the consequences, it threatens the balance, threatens the universe itself.

That's where people like me come in, people who can see the result of the tsunami before the butterfly is even born, who can nudge things back into order before everything collapses.

And that's why I'm sitting here, surrounded by dead bodies, being told I should be proud of myself.

It wasn't supposed to end like this, I swear. I just needed more butterflies.

◇

The balance had tipped towards chaos. We could all feel it, those of us tuned in to the magic flowing through our bodies, in infinite little ways. A wall now a different shade of blue, the name of a store suddenly spelled differently, historical events conflicting with our memories of them.

Time travel. It had to be time travel, someone going back and making changes that affected the present.

My hands flapped almost without effort on my part, the energetic movements sending twirling bursts of color from my fingertips. This was it, this was my chance to prove myself to Shelby and the other senior wizards.

I gathered up my research and ran down the halls of the office building. Yes, witches operate out of office buildings. It's the most efficient way to coordinate efforts to protect the universe. Not necessarily the most secretive way, but we performed a ritual every morning to keep up the glamour that made it look like an abandoned strip mall.

When I reached the big office, the senior witches were already talking about the changes. I listened in the doorway for a moment because nobody noticed me. It was clear they had no idea what they were dealing with.

"It's not pranksters," I said. The conversation stopped, and I looked at my feet to avoid eye contact as everyone turned to me.

"Mx. Grady," said Mr. Shelby, my boss. My boss's boss, technically. Somehow it was both a greeting and a dismissal.

"It's time travel," I continued, hesitatingly stepping inside and spreading my papers on a clear spot on the table. I tried not to let the irritated groans stop me. "It *is*. I've done the research. It's entirely possible someone could accidentally put the right spells together and—"

And they were all smirking at me. Because of me specifically, or because of the way they looked down at anyone who wasn't part of their fancy-schmancy elite team, I don't know. I try not to use mind-reading spells unless absolutely necessary.

"Time manipulation," one of them began, steepling his fingers because some book about nonverbal communication probably told him it would make him seem powerful, "is an extremely complicated process that takes years to master."

I stared at his forehead to suggest eye contact. "Teleportation and retrocognition," I said. "Combine those spells in just the right way, and you don't just see the past, you go there. And I'm not saying they've mastered it. I'm just saying they've done it." I pointed to my spreadsheets. "The data is all there."

I waited as they gave my research the most cursory of glances, wishing time manipulation was easier so I could skip the anxiety of waiting. I could do it. Theoretically, anyway.

Every cell in my body vibrated with potential magic power, I could feel it, but they never let me exercise it. Just stuck me with simple jobs, boring jobs. Don't get me wrong, I loved finding lost cats; it just didn't challenge me.

"It is plausible," Shelby conceded finally, reluctantly. It wasn't like him. He was never really interested in my ideas, but he usually at least pretended to be. "However, it is extremely unlikely and we cannot waste our resources chasing your wild time-traveling goose. We *will* not."

I tried hiding my devastation, but I've never been good at that kind of thing. "But what if I just...what if I did it myself?"

They all stared at me. I didn't have to cast a mind-reading spell to know they were all thinking the same thing: me? The office assistant who used their magic for refilling pens and finding cats?

I left before they could answer.

I left before they could answer, which meant, technically, they hadn't said no. I convinced myself that made it okay, and started the spells in the parking lot after everyone went home.

It's a bit like meditating, according to people with the patience to meditate. Controlling every breath, blocking out external stimuli until the only thing that exists is the magic.

I sensed it more than felt it, a constant force rippling across the universe and through my body. Like a diagram of a wind tunnel, I could see the way my every movement altered its flow, changed its course. Not by much, just a little flap of a butterfly wing, but if you do it just right, it becomes a tsunami.

It probably looked like I was dancing, the way I spun and thrust out my arms. It didn't feel like dancing. Dancing was free, joyful, letting my body move however it felt like moving. This was too precise, too rigid and calculated. Grabbing at the waves, twisting them just right and controlling my center of magic so as not to upset the balance.

History unfurled around me, just visible through the hazy curtain of my spell. I didn't have a destination in mind, I just followed my instincts and decades turned to centuries.

There. The eye of the storm.

I held up my hands, halting the rewinding vision in the early 1500s. Europe, it felt like Europe, but I couldn't get a great read on it beyond that. Too many distracting tsunamis radiating out from this time.

This is the part where I should have stopped, argued my case even harder the next day until someone took my idea seriously. But this is also the part where, through that misty, magical haze, I saw him. A man, dressed like the others around him and absolutely not distinctive in any way.

Purposely so, because he was using a glamour, disguising himself with magic. That didn't matter to me; I could practically smell the modern era on him, feel the pull of familiarity in his molecules.

I was right. Time travel.

I didn't think, I just jumped.

◇

The sheer power swirling around that little town...I'd never felt anything like it. Beautiful, full of potential, and so thick that I almost thought I'd suffocate.

That kind of thing, it doesn't happen naturally. Someone did that on purpose, and probably not with good intentions.

Conjuring a glamour for myself was easier than ever with that concentration of magic in the air. Just a little focus and a flick of the wrist, and I fit in with the rest of the French peasants. A flick of the other wrist and a little spin, and the language barrier shattered.

Yes, whoever he was, he was planning something big, something that needed an absurd amount of magic, and the effects would ripple outward for hundreds of years. All the way back to my time, changing the colors of walls and making Mr. Shelby act weird and who knows what else.

I don't know why I didn't go back for reinforcements. Fear of not being believed, maybe, or getting in trouble. Maybe I just really wanted to prove myself worthy of being in the big office with the elite witches.

I should have, I know that now and I think I knew it then. I wish I could change things, but I've seen the devastation playing around with time can cause. I won't do that, I won't become like him.

◇

Sometime during the jump from present to past, I lost sight of the mysterious man with the glamour. I could feel him, faintly, but extra magic in the air meant extra turbulence I wasn't used to dealing with.

So I wandered around without a real destination, hoping I would be able to sense him more clearly if I got closer. I followed a series of magical accidents through the town, a cute little village that looked like it should be animated and filled with people randomly bursting into song.

Alas, no spontaneous sing-alongs. But a lot of other curious occurrences—coincidences on top of coincidences, superstitious rituals creating impossibly good luck, even one report of a chicken turning bright blue.

I could not confirm the chicken incident, as the owner decided to charge people to see it and I had no intention of committing magical counterfeiting, but I don't doubt it was true. With that much power concentrated in one town, even people with a weak connection to magic could do amazing things without trying.

I hated to think what the clearly very powerful time traveler could do...but I would find out soon enough.

The closer I got to the Romanesque cathedral, already ancient even in the sixteenth century, the more I felt his presence. Like his ego came with a flashing neon sign. And the closer I got to the cathedral, apparently his base of operations, the stronger I felt his intentions.

Autistic people having no empathy, that's a myth. We have more of it than most, in my experience, we just don't always know what to do with it. I find it comes in handy for reading minds.

It isn't a perfect science, but it was enough for me to get a general idea of what he was trying to do.

The little changes we noticed back home? Those were practice, testing his powers to see if he could influence the distant future. His actual plan involved a lot more than changing the logo on a cereal box.

He meant to change everything, insert himself into all the great moments of history and install himself as some kind of immortal ruler.

I couldn't let that happen, but I didn't have anywhere near the control he did. If I tried anything, went directly against him in any way, he would overpower me. Especially with so much magic coursing through the town for him to draw from.

Unless... I found a way to use up a large portion of that magic before he could...

◇

Every step, every shake and twist reverberated through my body and the universe.

Until that moment, dancing my heart out in the middle of town in 1518, I had never really felt like I was part of it, of the balance and the butterflies and the magic. I used it, I lived it, I communicated with it, but it was separate from me.

No more. I couldn't even tell if I was guiding the magic or the magic was guiding me, we just danced as one.

It was a small spell that used up a lot of the ambient magic, but it didn't do much besides giving those nearby a little boost of energy and happiness.

The townsfolk joined me. Just a few at first, copying my moves without realizing they were tapping into their own innate magic, amplifying the effect of my spell. It drew more people in, dozens more, hundreds, all of us draining the surplus magic from the air.

We danced.

We danced, and we didn't stop, not even when the time traveler showed up, furious and nearly powerless now that we had used up his unnaturally stockpiled magic. He couldn't even keep up his glamour anymore.

Mr. Shelby.

It made sense, and it didn't make sense. Now I knew why he wouldn't even entertain the possibility. He didn't want me to discover what he was doing. But what exactly was he doing? Why? Didn't he believe in protecting people from this kind of abuse of magic?

I decided someone else could figure that out. My feet hurt from dancing, I just wanted to sit down and rest. After sending a message back to the office to have someone pick us up, anyway.

"See, I was right," I told my boss as he fumed, fumbling to conjure a way home. "Time travel."

He glared at me, but started involuntarily tapping his toes. Musicians had joined us, and gave a jaunty beat to our movements. Last I saw him, he was dancing away into the crowd.

Even when all the extra magic had been channeled into our spell and order reigned over chaos, people danced. It was joyous, dare I say magical. Nobody wanted to stop.

Nobody wanted to stop.

The rest of the senior wizards from the big office tell me it isn't my fault, that I saved history the only way I knew how. But even if it was Shelby's flapping wings that started it, my wings contributed to the tsunami. Made it smaller, maybe, but blew it towards victims who shouldn't have been in danger.

They danced themselves to exhaustion, the spell urging them to keep going even as their bodies gave out.

People died. A lot of people. Dozens of fragile butterflies crushed under the boot of a time traveler.

I'm going to try and set things right, but if you notice anything odd about the world in the next few days, sorry. Butterfly effect. Just accept it as a quirk of the chaotic nature of things, and maybe spare a thought to all the butterflies lost in other people's tsunamis.

This Way Lies Madness

Romy Tara Wenzel

Brother Frix, Red Hospital of St Anthony, Strasbourg, 6th August, 1518

The dancing victims kept me busy from lauds to vespers, which meant I neglected our sisters at the convent for some weeks. Sister Hilde had begged me to take some of their own manic patients in our larger, well-resourced infirmary, but Brother Ansgar was right: we couldn't have women inside the monastery.

This opinion was confirmed when I arrived at the convent to women in various states of undress: hair loose, collars open, unstockinged feet stamping the herbs and prancing through the violets. Several were herded by a frustrated nun with a stick, like goats. They were also as contrary as goats, each with their own impassioned direction, some howling with rage and protest in a paroxysm of dance, others faced heavenward in a kind of Bacchian ecstasy.

One woman emerged from the chapel, stripped to the waist. Sister Hilde's apprentice, Sparrow, appeared behind her, looking stricken, and received the woman's blouse in her face. The woman dashed across the garden, trampling leeks and bolted onions. I shielded my eyes, but nothing would ever erase that image of her, bare-breasted and laughing, running free in the garden.

I felt a touch on my cassock sleeve. Sister Hilde stood beside me, the sun on her face. Her brow was beaded with sweat and a few wiry gray hairs had escaped her wimple. In the harsh summer light she looked twenty years older, her face almost as creased as her habit. It was clear she'd slept in her clothes, if she'd slept at all. She didn't smile at me, and watched the half-naked woman climb an apple tree and fall out again with disinterest, as if she'd seen it a hundred times before.

"You've come to see the chaos for yourself," she said, in her matter-of-fact tone, but her voice was small and tired. "Good. I want you to know what you're refusing us. Etiquette should not apply in times of plague." I took the path towards the infirmary, but Sister Hilde turned on her heel towards the refectory.

The noise I'd expected. My own hospital was a veritable symphony of screams from dancing men hallucinating rivers of blood, hellfire and dragons. What I did not expect was the stench. The smell of illness emanated from the refectory like infirmary sheets unchanged for weeks, and I had an urgent need to retch. I copied the sisters hurrying inside, and covered my nose with my handkerchief.

There were fewer dancers inside than outside, but those who danced produced more chaos, moving inelegantly between, and sometimes over the patients in the beds. From the looks of the shards on the floor, they hadn't spared the plates, either, and I noted that lunch was served up in wooden bowls. Patients were passed out both on top of and underneath the tables, with only a thin layer of straw or a sheet underneath them.

There were open wounds, and I could see a barber making the rounds to tend to amputations, using no sedative. The air was thick with the stinking breath of unclean mouths, and blood, and soiled clothes and linens.

I was horrified to see sisters in the kitchen, preparing meals in the same space as the sick. They didn't serve them as part of a formal meal, but were sending them out as they were spooned, and a sister brought each bowl to anyone capable of being fed. It was like the hospital campsite of a battlefield.

"You can't serve food here!" I exclaimed. "Why aren't these patients in the infirmary?"

"There are plenty of patients in the infirmary, as well as everywhere else," Hilde said dryly. "We try to keep the dancers outside until they collapse or need sedation, but if they've a mind to come in here, we don't have the numbers to stop them."

"But why aren't you using something for the pain?" I cried, as the shriek of a patient cut through the air.

"The barber can't wait for direction from the sisters, who more often than not are chasing down dancers a danger to themselves and others. We try to corral them in the chapel, but they frequently escape. You turn women away for the sake of etiquette, but sometimes etiquette comes second to the work that must be done. I am glad you could see our situation with your own eyes. Perhaps the truth will sway you from bad influences."

"You mean Ansgar." Brother Ansgar's arrival had coincided with the influx of dancing patients, and he'd already proved himself invaluable despite being the newest addition to my infirmary hands and losing five fingers to gangrene. "Don't you trust me to make my own decisions?"

Hilde assessed me. I suspected she wasn't capable of holding her tongue, even if she wanted to.

"I think you are too influenced by pretty...words."

Sparrow laughed, and a blush crept into my cheeks. Ansgar and I had something special between us, something I'd never experienced with another brother. He made me question my assumptions, held me accountable for my decisions. He was convinced the plague was a punishment from God that could only be purged through suffering; I argued that it was a disorder of the mind, and we'd had many spirited, late-night conversations trying to win each other over. Instead of dividing us, our shared confidence had made obvious our care for each other. Now I feared it had been observed. Hilde gave Sparrow a steely look and Sparrow turned the laugh into a cough.

"Ansgar is handsome and mysterious, to be sure," Hilde continued. "He's suffered, although no more than any Alsatian peasant. He's no saint, nor martyr, however much he might wish to be, and his passions will lead him astray. You must tread carefully, Frix, or they will lead you astray, too. Choose allies who appeal to your mind, as well as your heart."

I felt my color rise. "My allies are my brothers, my order is my family. It's not God's will that I should choose favorites."

"Lie to me if you need to save face, Frix. But don't lie to yourself."

I had no words, but Hilde seemed satisfied with my expression. We strolled back to the meditation walk in silence. As we left the refectory, I took a last look and had a glimpse of the glinting saw of the barber in the open doorway.

I swallowed. The images were collecting behind the closed door in my mind, my training with the barber-surgeon Krause that I tried hard to keep at bay; the clamps, hooks, knives and saws. I put a hand over my eyes and sat down, slowing my breath as the abbot had taught me to do. I bolted the lock and turned away from that mind-door; it couldn't be opened under any circumstances.

But then, inside the refectory, a saw squeaked against bone. I leaned into the unkempt hedge, my hands tearing on the brambles. Hilde didn't turn away, as a more discreet companion might have, but watched me, unflinching, as I vomited up my boiled oats. She said not a word, but snapped off a sprig of peppermint between the stones on the path, crushed the leaves, and handed it to me. I took the peppermint, but didn't hold it to my nose to disguise the smell, as some of the other nuns did. I walked the path with my head high, the mint spurned in my hand, inhaling the reek of illness and death. I would take it all in. I would not avert my eyes from breasts or surgeon's saws, or disguise the reek of illness with peppermint nosegays. I'd look death in the eye, and I would not hesitate to do what had to be done.

I hurried back to the monastery, the sky bruised violet and swollen with clouds. The door in the gate was closed. St Anthony's hadn't been closed in the abbot's lifetime. As I drew close, my own apprentice, Phillipe, arrived back from the market with a basket on his arm.

"What are you doing out here, Master Frix?"

"This door is only closed in times of war. Something is wrong. Be quiet, Phillipe," I said, and put my ear to a knothole. I was not mistaken: there were noises coming from inside, as if from a muffled room. I tried to see through the hole, but the summer-bolted greenery blocked the view. Suddenly a scream cut through the air and was cut short, and Phillipe grabbed my sleeve.

The latch moved on the other side of the door, and then paused, as if the person on the other side were listening.

"Brother?" I asked quietly, through the knothole. "It's Frix. What has happened?"

"Frix! Thank goodness!" Brother Knapp flung the door open. "By the heavens, Frix, they've all gone mad."

I caught him by his vestments.

"What's going on in there, Knapp? Is it safe for us to come in?" I shook him when he didn't answer, and a horrible thought occurred to me. "Has the mania spread through the brothers?"

Knapp shook his head. His eyes were ringed with white. I could smell the sweat on him, not of summer, but of fear. "A group of brothers say the dancing is God's punishment and they are His wrath. They're breaking the dancers' legs. Let me go, Frix. Let me pass! We must all of us flee!"

I plunged past Knapp through the gate and up the path, my feet carrying me towards whatever disaster awaited, Phillipe on my heels.

At first I thought they were dead, seeing my patients stretched out in the cloisters and the brothers gathered around them like mourners. But as we neared the scene, I saw some lay writhing, their legs at awful angles, screaming at the pain of not being able to stop their motion, while others seemed to have stopped their convulsions altogether. Disappointingly few monks tended to the ones that would allow it, soothing them, binding their legs, cutting bandages and splints.

I threw myself down next to Cheval, a patient who had been dancing for two weeks. He looked up at me, his legs at angles all wrong, his wheat-coloured hair awry with sticks and dirt, his eyes wide and trusting. "I'm cured!" he said, too loudly to be entirely convincing. "Cured!" He looked around, as if expecting his announcement to be echoed amongst the other victims on the battlefield. Then, the shock of the pain set in, and he curled up over his legs, writhing slowly against the ground like an unearthed worm.

"What happened here, Cheval?" I asked him, but he only moaned, holding his knees, his head rocking from side to side.

I felt eyes on me and looked up, blinking back the tears.

Brother Ansgar was standing at a distance, watching the chaos with a mild expression. He leaned on a wooden staff, fashioned from an oak branch. The eleven brothers that stood with him held similar branches, all sanded smooth so they wouldn't splinter or blister their hands. Ansgar held his awkwardly, his hands wrapped around the staff like paws, but from the gleam in his eye I suspected, despite his deformed hands he'd been able to swing the weapon competently enough.

I felt a new callous form around my heart. Ansgar did this. Ansgar, who I'd trusted, my most beloved brother. *His passions will lead him astray.* Hilde could not have known how soon. Even now I yearned to make him see sense, to make him an ally, not an enemy, to have him by my side, on the winning side in the war against darkness. But he'd made his choice, and although it stung me to do so, I turned my back on him.

If I must choose between my dearest brother and my humanity, I chose my humanity.

I told Phillipe to get all the men to the infirmary, what herbs to collect, the medicines to prepare, and began the bandaging. If we'd had opium to spare, I suspect I would've used it myself to retire from the nightmare.

◇

Andreas Drachenfels, the Ammeister of Strasbourg, sat on his chair as if it were a throne. He was tall and fat. His buttons were made of mother-of-pearl shells, the curling iridescent spiral in them reminding me of maggots I'd seen in battle-wounds.

"Brother," he said, smiling in a mocking way. "Will you take some brandy? I take a little to cheer me, at this time of day. My constitution tends towards the melancholic."

"Thank you, but no." I perched upon the large chair, made for considerably larger buttocks than mine.

"Ah yes. Deprivation is the mark of your order, is it not?"

"I would not have said so, but deprivation during times of strife can keep one's thoughts in order. Chaos is the enemy of order."

"Ah, order. Yes. Order is the hallmark of your order, heh. I was thinking of the Franciscans. I lose track of which cassock means what."

"We are all God's servants, no matter the color of our cassock."

He turned a button, his eyes not shifting from mine.

"Never mind, never mind. I want no theological quarrels here. Tell me why you've come, Brother Frix."

"I think you must know the abbot has been very unwell these last months. What you may not know is that a new monk took advantage of the abbot's absence to divide the brothers in service to his misled cause. This brother sanctioned horrendous violences on the dancers in our care; those we promised to heal and protect. He has made things infinitely worse, for the dancers, and for those of us who take care of them. He must be held accountable for his actions and removed from St Anthony's."

The ammeister nodded seriously, and I felt hope. "We mustn't allow things to escalate. Tell me what happened."

I told him about the convent being overrun with patients, about the men laid out like broken dolls, but even though I had intended to, I did not mention Ansgar's name. A part of me wanted to protect him, to believe that he had not done this on purpose.

"I arrived too late, and the damage was already done. That they kept it quiet is testimony to the influence he wields with the brothers, none of whom said a thing. It's madness. They injured anyone affected by the mania, and anyone who stood in their way."

The ammeister leaned forward, interested. "And did it work?" he said, settling his chin on his fingers.

"Did it...work? How could it *work?* Many stopped dancing, to be sure, because I have them sedated under opium until their broken and stitched legs can heal...if they're one of the lucky ones. Two or three came to their senses, and moan and cry from their beds; one will not walk again. So, I would say, Ammeister, that it did not work."

The ammeister leaned back and took a sip from his cup, which had small pearls set into the side.

"To be frank, we've considered similar measures. We even experimented, but as the patient continued to dance, we found ourselves in a more awkward position than to begin with. Tending wounds on the feet of someone while they're thrashing about is one thing, but someone who writhes about on cobblestones on their back or God forbid, their face...well, it's an even less pretty picture than the one we are faced with. So when Brother Ansgar came to me with this experiment..."

"You sanctioned this violence?"

"It was a way of containing the experiment."

The experiment. I realized, suddenly, this was a mistake. That by coming, I'd cemented the ammeister's support of Ansgar's methods.

"Even if it were true what Ansgar says," I said, barely containing the tremor in my voice, "and they were sinners in need of penitence, are they not already punished enough by the dance? Their feet bleed, their limbs ache, they cry of fire and flames and are tortured by hallucinations...their tendons were already torn to the bone, just from exertion. By any hypothesis, they've been through enough."

The ammeister stroked the leather inlay on his desk with two fingers, and moved to his wrist, stroking his unsunned skin as if he were checking for a pulse.

"You've told me yourself some of the patients woke from their spell," the ammeister said. "Are you able to provide me with better options, Brother Frix?"

He looked at me, his gentle, cow-like eyes utterly calm, and I could see he didn't care if a hundred legs were broken, if it would stop the paperwork and the scandal.

"Take them to the chapel at Saverne. Take them out of the city. While they dance before all, they will continue to take root in the popular imagination. The dancer who started it all, Frau Troffea, was healed by St Vitus there, and it will get them out of the public gaze."

And that of Ansgar and his allies, I added silently.

The ammeister blinked, lazily. "Many of these people are peasants. They cannot afford a chapel pilgrimage."

"Tell their guilds to pay, if they belong to one. If not, let the council fund it. Or I am afraid you'll be facing a situation beyond your guards. Will you be the ammeister who backed the violence against already broken people, or saved the city in a time of crisis?" The ammeister put his glass down, and was watching me with more attention. "Fund a share of the expenses to Saverne, Ammeister, and it will all go away."

The ammeister sighed. "I'll speak with the Twenty-One. But Brother Ansgar will remain at the monastery, and continue to have a say in how the patients are treated. The abbot is too soft-hearted. Measures must be taken for the city's interest, not the individual. There will be no more broken legs…for the present, until we can better assess the ramifications. You have a reprieve, but I can promise no more."

He poured himself more brandy. "You've added to my melancholy, Brother Frix," he said, cradling his glass.

Melancholy is not your problem, I almost said. *You are full of black bile and your heart is cold.* Despite my habits, despite my training, I could have said it, considered saying it. But I knew this man would easily hurt people out of spite, and I bit my tongue for their sake.

The ammeister picked up his quill, and began to scratch some letters in a ledger. Assuming I was dismissed, I stood up and left, not bothering to take my leave. He'd given me a promise with so many caveats it meant nothing.

When I left the building it was evening, and the lamp-lighters were already out with their torches. There was a change in the air; a wind was quickening. The long buildings cast amber shadows down the street, and the faces of the people taking the cool night air glowed in the last light, like the world was on fire.

◇

I found the infirmary door locked. I searched my belt for the key, my hands trembling. It had been a long time since I'd needed it, since the infirmary had always been left unlocked. Everything had been kept unlocked, until Ansgar came.

I fitted the key to the lock and pushed the door open.

Ansgar stood on the workbench, a crown of thorns on his head, small red rivers running down from the points where the thorns broke the skin. His eyes were shining, his face radiant. Several of the 'cured' dancing patients knelt on broken knees before him in a strange, sweating ecstasy of prayer, their mouths shaping letters in a rapture. Cheval smiled as he whispered into clasped hands, although the floor beneath him was black with the blood leaking through his bandages.

"What...what are you doing, Ansgar?" I whispered, afraid to startle him as he poured a spoonful of thick syrup from a bottle, and fed it to a novice kneeling beside the broken men. I recognised the bottle; of course I did. There were only ten such in the apothecary, small and glinting with the poppy juice inside. "You'll poison yourselves!"

"I don't feel poisoned," said Ansgar, "but filled with light from heaven. The Swiss elixir brings one to the very threshold of truth. I see clearly now, what is to be done to end this nightmare, Frix. We must take their suffering upon ourselves; burn their sins away with mortifications of the flesh."

"Stop," I said, alarmed. I made my way carefully between the patients, some of them with their hands clasped and eyes rolling, others snoring soundly with their faces buried in the straw. There were scatterings of broken glass on the floor, and dark wet splashes of the tincture on the tiles between the rushes. "Opium can only be used at full dose, for sedation. Half-doses lead to madness, to visions."

"Did St Anthony not have visions? And Jesus? Did God not make the poppy, alongside all the other flowers?"

Ansgar caressed the novice's cheek. "Are you ready, my son?" The boy looked at him through doe-eyes, a drop of black tincture still on his bottom lip, like a milk-drunk infant looking adoringly at its mother. Ansgar raised his other hand, and my surgeon's scalpel glinted between the thumb and the forefinger. "Put the smallest finger of your left hand on the bench."

The novice obliged. His thin white finger shook so badly it made the nettle on the bench shiver.

"Don't you see this is as deranged as the physicians who urge them to dance?" I raged, unable to temper the fury in my voice. "To cut away parts of a man that are perfectly well in the name of healing is a terrible crime."

"Suffering, more than anything else, makes present in the history of humanity the powers of the Redemption," Ansgar said, his voice high and quavering, quoting Saint Paul as he marked a cross on his forehead with the heel of the scalpel. "Since not all can pay the price of their penance, we take on their suffering, as Christ took our suffering into His own hands."

Quick as a thief, I pinched the blade from his grasp and flicked the knife around at Ansgar. Ansgar stumbled backwards, clutching the bench to steady himself. He knocked over the nine-hour candle, and it fell onto the straw of the bed below, where some of the opium tincture had spilled. In a trice, the soaked straw burst into flame, spitting out heat and forcing us back.

I looked in horror as the fire hungrily consumed the straw, rising in red and orange tongues and searching for something else on which to feed as it found splashes of tincture around the foot of the bed. My mind snapped into focus.

The empty bed was set away from the others; if it was put out immediately, it could be contained.

"A blanket!" I shouted to Ansgar, but he was watching the fire with an infuriating tranquility on his face, as absorbed in the flames as if he read a premonition in them. His acolytes, kneeling on the floor, looked around and stared at the rising flames dumbly, mesmerized. There was a clatter of bowls and plates as Phillipe, who had appeared at the door, dropped the tray of food in his hands. Phillipe did not need to be told, but ran for help. I stumbled over to the beds and grasped the broom by the door, shouting into the night as I passed, "Fire in the infirmary! Buckets, blankets! Fire! Fire!"

I tried to beat the flames with the broom, but it only fanned them in a new direction. The rising smoke had a delicious flavor, like the earthy notes of the kitchen's oven after Cook baked the refectory bread. I tried to shake the patients from their stupor. The flames crackled merrily as they found new timbers to chew on.

"Ansgar!" I screamed. "Help Cheval and the others. Drag them, if you must. Never mind their legs, it's their lives at stake. We must get everyone out, before the beds catch!"

Phillipe returned with a stretcher and men. I directed them to the patients with the worst injuries, helped roll one onto the canvas as the man woke and began to dance, dragged patients from their beds, heedless of their screams.

I struggled to pull Cheval to his feet. He resisted me, even beat his hands on my thighs. I was stronger than him, and wrenched him off his knees. His legs straightened with a sickening crunch and he fainted, collapsing in a heap on the flagstones like a slaughtered goat.

"You must not take the sacrifices!" a voice howled, and Ansgar flew towards me, his robes swirling about him like black plumes. He hit me with the full force of his body, knocking the wind from me, and I slipped backwards and caught his long sleeve as he fell. He wrapped his legs around my waist, grappled with the cloth of my cowl, and the strange sticks of his fingers found my throat. We wrestled, grappling at each other as if we were climbing, our arms, our thighs, fighting for dominance. I found my feet and sprang at him. There was a sickening crunch as his head hit the corner of the bench. My own hit the flagstones, hard, and I saw stars.

As if in a dream, I sat up and watched as the brothers ran around like strange ants bustling around a disruption to their nest. One brother hustled those with unbroken legs from their beds and chased them to the door, flapping his arms and screaming.

The beds were alight. They burned fast and hot, and I tried to shy away from them, but my head screamed with the movement. Ansgar was lying still, his eyes closed, blood trickling from his temple into his hair.

The air around us was thick with fire, and my head was light from smoke. The flames were climbing the walls, catching the herbs that hung from the roof, and I shouted to Ansgar. I knew what would happen when the heat reached the distilling glasses on the high shelf. I threw myself to the ground and covered my face as the glass tinkled in a thousand shards on the floor around me. When I opened my eyes Ansgar was lying with his head turned towards me, his cheek against stone, his clear eyes on mine, his face wiped of all anger, all worry. The glass had crosshatched red lines across his face, and the blood welled under the surface. Dully, I watched as Phillipe and the others helped the last patients from the building behind him.

Ansgar's hand crept over the flagstones towards mine, and laced his three fingers in mine.

"You would have let them burn?" I whispered, as the flames grew higher and the flames flickered over the crucified Christ on the wall.

"I would have saved them all," he said. My hand grew heavier in the warmth of his, and when he felt my commitment his fingers closed around mine. "But I would save you, Frix, over any of them."

I held on to his hand, barely registering Phillipe, covered in a wet woolen blanket, grunting as he slid his small arms under mine and dragged me to my feet. I tightened my fingers, but Ansgar gently released his, and Phillipe pulled me away.

The flames were blazing across almost all the beds now, and there was no way out. I watched as the *Ship of Fools* print by the door curled to black in a matter of seconds. Another lot of herbs hanging from the ceiling caught alight, and the fire raced over the sage, the calendula, the rosemary. When the flames hit the apothecary, Ansgar was doomed; it was stocked with alcohol, dried plants and animal fat.

"Take off your cloak!" I cried, choking on the smoke. "Ansgar, smother the flames with your cloak! Get to the door!" Ansgar pulled himself to the edge of the table and fumbled to unlatch his cloak. In the awkwardness of undressing, his elbow knocked over the bottle of rubbing alcohol used to make tinctures. The glass smashed on the floor, and the fire roared, hiding Ansgar's expression behind a wall of flames.

My scorched throat gulped down the air outside, although it was thick with smoke and made me cough up black phlegm into my hand. I looked around, mad with the chaos, and took in several images, surreal as paintings.

Patients seemed to float through the air on stretchers, the brothers carrying them hidden by the swirling smoke. Some stared up at the building in a kind of stupor, while industrious brothers made a line to pass buckets of water from the refectory, and threw them in the windows of the building. The abbot hobbled over to release the bolt on the two strong-gates, and they caught on the wind, smacking against the stones and echoing through the courtyard.

Sparrow and several nurses ran inside the gate, and suddenly a stream of women from the annex came dancing past the blazing infirmary. The dancers gathered in the cloister garden, unfazed by the smoke and the fire, jerking and thrusting their hips among the roses. The men who had been carried out with broken legs writhed like worms in the grass, and one of the women began to wail. Others joined the first, like the lamentations of harpies in Dante's hell.

Some of my brothers, who clustered around the door to the infirmary, tried to push their way inside, but were forced back by the heat and flame.

"Ansgar," I said weakly. "Ansgar is inside."

One brother began to scream as the flames burned brighter and hotter, and others joined in. Their wails rose on the smoke and filled the air as if they were part of the sacrifice. The rosemary hedge by the door had caught alight and was making a furnace, sucking the fire from the infirmary and threatening to provide a bridge to the other buildings.

I took a bucket from a brother who was beginning to fatigue. The water sloshed on my arms and evaporated on my skin before I even had a proper hold on the handle, and I hurled the contents at the infirmary, and then a full bucket was passed to me, and then another, as fast as I could empty them.

They grew heavier each time, as if it wasn't buckets I was carrying, but corpses, and it seemed to go on and on as if the inferno would never stop. At last I began to sway on my feet, and Phillipe pulled me away from the building. I stumbled towards the garden, the garden of healing powers, that held prayer and peace and quiet. I fell into the poppies, and my mind closed up like a book.

The flames, the patients, the monks throwing water at the smoldering building, all fell away, and there was only patterns of the smoke tracing the breeze in the sky above me, and the cool earth below me, and the ringing in my ears, although I knew the bells could not be ringing at such a time.

And there was Ansgar.

I closed my eyes to remember his face as he had lain opposite me on the flagstones, his fingers entwined in mine. His face was holy, lit from within, his eyes shining with love. There'd been no trace of hatred or fear in his eyes, only the clear eyes of my brother, looking at me with sublime grace. His eyes leaked as a cloud, the tears gathering at his lashes and spilling over that carved cheek, and he'd smiled through his tears, and his teeth had been covered in blood.

The sky thickened with black clouds, and the grounds were dark as night. A supernatural mist lingered from the smoldering remains of the hospital, sucked the green from all the plants and trees, making everything a uniform gray, and the silhouettes of the monks ghostly and vague.

There was a small cheer over from the infirmary; the fire was out. The fragments of glass from the smashed windows had melted away, and the rosemary bushes underneath them were only black cinders. There was nothing left to burn. I began to breathe short and fast. I was tired of it all, tired of the pain, the loss, the betrayal, the holding back. I couldn't bear to hold the emotions back any longer. It was too much for one man to hold. The seas inside me rose.

Thunder cracked the night open. The wind rustled the bolted coriander, sending a sprinkling of seed through the bed. The dancers, in the cloistered garden, moved with gathering intensity, rising and falling like the heartbeat of the earth.

It was too much, and the last straw of my mind snapped.

I felt my feet carrying me away, drifting to the cloisters where the dancers were moving with the chaos, embracing it as a shifting current through their bodies, amplifying it, ecstasy on their faces as they whirled around like dervishes. The cloud cover drifted over them, their shadows sharpened and softened against the kept grass of the square in rhythm to the drum that pounded over and over, like the heartbeat of the earth. But there was no drum, only the footfall of the dancers as I hovered on the edge of their circle, so hypnotizing, so inviting.

The wood battered the hinges of the gates in the wind, loosening the iron nails one by one. Hilde and Ansgar had both tried to fight the plague, to resist it. But history had much to teach on resistance. Resistance had been drawn many times over by the people in the rage-filled uprisings of history, and those in power had resisted them with violence. Traditional resistance ended in bloodshed. If we were to resist, it would have to be an overhauled, new resistance...a resistance based in peace, in eloquence, a lyrical resistance.

A resistance, to be precise, that looked exactly like how it had manifested in the people of Strasbourg. Their surrender to the dance *was* their resistance. Resistance to hunger, to poverty, to an unjust system.

It came to me in that clear, sharp thought, transcending Hilde's outrage and Ansgar's delusions. The answer was softening, absorbing, becoming; running as a river, joining to the flow, becoming what already was.

Their surrender is their resistance.

It sang in my bones, in my blood, rose like a tide within, sang out and over my terror and regret.

There was only the dance. The dance said it all.

The infirmary smoldered as the brothers and sisters continued to throw water over the dampening flames. Billows of black smoke clouded the air, stinging the eyes and obscuring the sky. A cheer went up among the brethren. I saw Phillipe and Sparrow, collapsed by the church wall side by side, their heads bowed towards each other as they caught their breath.

The infirmary was no more. Ansgar was no more. To this I must surrender.

The surrender is the resistance.

I let the closed door in my mind open, the door that all medical men keep locked and bolted. I heard a terrible screaming, the high-pitched voice of a woman, and on the other side another scream, a man this time. Other voices joined in, a chorus of all the patients I'd ever had screaming at once, until I realized with horror their screams were coming from my own mouth. I clapped my hands over my mouth and squeezed my eyes shut as they crawled among the dancers, amputated limbs, burst bellies and all. Hot and salty tears fell down my face as I begged them in their own voices to go back behind the door, and then all of a sudden something snuck into my hand. I squeezed it, and recognised his fingers, so hard and brittle I feared they would crumble in my fist. But memories didn't crumble, and Ansgar's hand curled up in mine until the warmth of his palm cupped my own, two hands intertwined, and that union gave me the courage to open my eyes. Patients I'd not seen for ten years or more, patients who were long dead, gathered around me like neglected children, and I found I wasn't afraid of them anymore, but caressed their faces and joined hands with them to dance.

The skies opened, and the rain fell, heavy and cool on our faces. The dancers blinked and threw their heads back and opened their mouths and closed their eyes. The roses seemed to be alive, writhing in the rain. The faces became a blur as they spun, roses and faces together, and I found my body following as if I were a clock wound tight and my cogs and wheels programmed to spin in their center. I heard a drum, or many, and I couldn't tell if it was the feet of the dancers, or my own feet, or my heart that pounded so insistently in my chest.

I felt a glorious freedom and release, my head empty of fear and my body free from suffering. I felt closer to God than ever, as the world spun and filled with wet smoke, and my chest was tight and laughter spilled over the cloisters, effortless as rain.

The bells began to ring.

The Consequences of Sin

JD Byrne

Bob and Val were not hiding. A demon of Bob's talent did *not* hide. He didn't care what his colleagues might say, they were just jealous. He'd accomplished so much in his youth, demonically speaking. Nonetheless, he had agreed with Val that there was some value in not making themselves too easy to find. After their fun in Strasbourg it made sense to be incognito, which is why they were holed up in this barn on the banks of the Rhine. Humans could be persistent, but they were easy to fool.

"You're being paranoid," he said to Val from the loft. "If you don't relax, you're going to miss out on this." He held up one of the farmer's chickens he'd caught, so fresh the blood was still pumping.

"Not hungry," the succubus said as she peeked out the cracked barn door. "Don't see how you can be."

"I don't see how you can't be," he said, "after all that excitement."

"All that excitement is what's going to get us in trouble."

"Us? You mean me," Bob said after taking another bite of the warm, throbbing bird. "This was all down to me, you know that."

"I goaded you into it," Val said, turning to look up at him. "I always do. Besides, you think the cardinal is the kind to draw fine distinctions?"

He smiled. "You do bring out the best in me. But there's nothing to worry about. I did what our kind do, corrupted the corruptible. So the simple humans got caught up in something, and it succeeded beyond my wildest dreams. It won't be the last time, you know that."

"I never should have pushed you," she said. "It got too big."

"Well, you did and that's done. Now, if you don't get up here and help me finish off this meal, you're going to have to catch one of the foul things yourself."

She sighed, took one last look outside, then climbed up into the loft. She sat down across from Bob and held out her hand.

"You've never been one to put in the work," he said, smirking, and handing over what was left of the chicken.

She didn't answer, instead sinking her teeth into the bloody mess. After she'd swallowed the first bite, she said, "I think we've given the humans the slip. I hope I never see that cardinal again."

He nodded. "Maybe we can get some rest, then? We've been on the move constantly for the last couple of weeks."

"One of us should stay up and take watch, though," she said, ripping off another hunk of flesh.

"I hereby nominate you to the position," he said, stretching out and lying down in the soft hay.

Bob awakened to the sound of muffled voices and footsteps on the dry grass outside. He knew instantly that it wasn't Val, since she was sprawled in the hay right next to him, in the best imitation of human intimacy they could muster. She didn't stir.

Shafts of moonlight pierced the gaps between the poorly hewn boards that made up the barn's wall. The light disappeared then reemerged, as if someone had walked in front of the moon.

He put his hand over Val's mouth and whispered, "Wake up. We've got company."

"Who?" she said, muffled.

"Probably the damned cardinal and his men," he said. He toyed with the idea that it was just animals. They were on a farm, after all, and the beasts were everywhere. Was he the one turning paranoid now?

Then he heard voices again. There was more than one speaker, definitely, but Bob still couldn't make out what was being said.

"Somebody's definitely outside," he whispered as Val sat up.

"Humans?" she asked.

"I ass..." Bob started to say, before a familiar voice rang out.

"Bobzolach the Tempter," the cool, bass voice said. "And Valgrelaath the Seductress. There is nowhere for you to run anymore."

"Shit," Bob said, panic quickly giving way to resignation. "It's worse than humans. It's Olvauz."

$$\diamond$$

The room was long and slender, with a rugged ceiling thirty feet above. It was drafty, as you'd expect of an aging castle where you could see hints of moonlight leaking in through the cracks of the stone block walls. Candles in tall stands around the corners of the room gave just enough light to see. On the floor was the wreckage of a narrow table that once must have been truly impressive. Now the only function it served was to divide the parties to whatever this proceeding was.

Bob stood on one side. Next to him was Gagthul, a demon with smooth black skin who had been assigned as Bob's advocate. Bob didn't suspect that the advocate's heart, or what would pass for one, was in it, but at least he was here. On the other side was Olvauz, whose voice had filled Bob with such dread. It had been Olvauz who initiated Bob into his role as a tempter, a harvester of souls. He was older than Bob could even imagine and had seen so much. He'd seen The Fall. His pale skin threw into sharp contrast the deep, dark eyes where, sometimes, you could see the flames of hell itself blazing.

There were four others with him, none of whom Bob had seen before. One was a demon with a mouth so big it was like his head was in danger of being swallowed by teeth. A second demon had no mouth at all, the smallest of noses, and large black eyes. There was a succubus too, with whom Bob had spent a wild weekend in Milan. The final member of this ad-hoc council was a small being with pointed ears sticking straight out from its head. Bob thought it might be an imp and wondered what it meant that Olvauz couldn't even round out his council with proper demons.

On the floor next to Olvauz was a small box made of dark wood. It was about the size of a human head and was covered in carvings. From this distance, Bob thought they were runes or some kind of text, rather than images, but it was hard to tell.

Standing off to the side, just behind the imp, was Val. She held her hands clasped in front of her, keeping her gaze mostly on the floor. She looked up once, catching Bob's glance, but otherwise avoided any eye contact.

Bob decided there was no need to delay things any more. "This one told me what this is all about." He nodded toward Gagthul. "But I still don't understand it."

"What is it you don't understand?" Olvauz asked.

"Why anyone thinks I did something wrong," Bob said. "It was a standard tempting, with a little of my personal spin. Isn't that what we're supposed to do, tempt the humans?"

"To sin, as singular entities who risk their own soul," Olvauz said. "We are not supposed to create mass events over which we have no real control."

"So I've been dragged here for being too efficient?" He chuckled. "You're all jealous that I could do it. Especially the *way* I did it."

"Yes," Olvauz said, "how did you do it? To make so many dance?"

Bob glanced at Val. She looked up, then quickly away, and he knew she'd told them all this already. There was nothing to hide. "I found a woman, Frau Troffea, who was profoundly unhappy with her life. She wanted nothing more than freedom, liberation, from her dull drudgery. When I asked if she liked music, she said she did and had a great memory for folk songs. That was the open door I needed."

"How did you walk through it?" asked the imp.

"I once heard a song, played by herders in the Carpathian mountains. The rhythm was so insistent, so infectious, that it drove anyone who heard it to dance," Bob explained. "Even me, briefly. She couldn't resist it."

"You played it for her?" the demon with no mouth asked, somehow.

Bob grinned and put his finger to his forehead. "I put it in her head, directly into her mind. She alone could hear it. She can't help but dance, yet no one else hears the tune or can figure why. Brilliant, right?"

There was some murmuring among the other demons, although Olvauz did not join in. Bob was right to think they would be impressed.

"Then how did it spread?" Olvauz finally asked, after the din died down.

Bob shrugged. "I don't know. The human mind is so odd and broken, who knows why they do what they do half the time?"

Before anyone else could ask another question, Gagthul spoke up. "I think what is important to consider here is that Bobzolach's conduct was limited to a single person, this Frau Troffea. He cannot be held responsible for anything that happened to anyone else."

Bob nodded in agreement.

"You did not intend that anyone should die?"

"Kill humans?" Bob recoiled. Tempting and stealing souls was their aim, not death. That would always come soon enough. "I have more talent and subtlety than that." He turned to Gagthul and whispered, "People died?"

Olvauz answered the question. "There are reports of deaths, as many as fifteen a day, by some accounts. Tell me, had you ever attempted something like this before, Bobzolach?"

"No, I..." Bob started, then stopped, unable to keep from looking at Val.

"Don't worry about Valgrelaath," Olvauz said, without moving. "She's been very helpful with her recollections. Trying to hide her role in all this due to some misguided notion of chivalry won't do her any good. Or you, for that matter."

Bob decided to cut to the chase. "If you already know why I did the thing in Strasbourg, then what is this all about?"

"Yes, we know that you and Val had an argument about who was the more subtle tempter, isn't that right?"

"Pfft," Bob said, waving away the idea. "Succubi have it so much easier, tempting men into carnal degradation. No offense." He nodded toward the succubus on the council. "I knew I was better, and I proved it."

"Did you ever think of the consequences of proving that boast?" Olvauz's voice was getting fuller, richer with each word.

"That I would have another human's soul and prove that I was the better tempter," Bob said, folding his arms.

"What about the unintended consequences?" Olvauz asked, slowly.

Bob didn't answer immediately.

Suddenly, Olvauz grew to three times his regular size, glowering down on Bob with the fires of damnation in his eyes. Bob had done a similar trick a few times to humans, and he did not like being on the receiving end. "The unintended consequences!"

That was it. Bob was done letting Olvauz or anyone else try to intimidate him. "I am a demon!" Bob shouted. "We're all demons," he said, then nodded toward the imp. "Except for him."

The imp pouted.

"Demons are tempters of humanity," Bob continued. "Our role in the universe is to seduce them into sin, to bring them one step closer to everlasting torment. Those were the intended consequences of my actions in Strasbourg and anything else is irrelevant. You just can't stand that I thought of it first."

"He is young," said the demon with no mouth.

"Does he not know about Aachen?" said the succubus.

"Aachen?" Bob said. "I've been to Aachen many times. It's not so special."

"It was a century-and-a-half ago," Olvauz said, returning to the usual presentation of himself. "Did you think you were the first to have the idea of driving a human to dance interminably? In Aachen in 1374 a demon named Xogmorech did the same thing. Like you, he implanted something in the head of a hapless woman, but could not stop the spread of the madness to hundreds of others."

"I suppose you gave him some kind of award?" Bob said, smirking. "I would like to meet Xogmorech, perhaps compare notes."

"That would be quite impossible," Olvauz said. "Xogmorech was slain."

If demons had blood, Bob's would have run cold. Humans sometimes assumed that demons were immortal, but the truth was their existence could be snuffed out quite easily, with the right knowledge and determination. "A human did that?"

"Yes," Olvauz said. "But she didn't get to Xogmorech first. She took almost a half dozen of our kind before she was put in the ground."

"Why does he not know this?" the imp asked. "All who dwell in the dark places know of Aachen."

"We have been too lenient with our younger brethren," said the demon of teeth, glancing at Olvauz.

"Stop!" Olvauz yelled. His voice echoed off the stone walls for what seemed like an eternity. "We are here to discuss Bobzolach's conduct, nothing more. One should not need specific training to avoid disasters like Aachen...or Strasbourg."

"Disaster?" Bob turned to Gagthul. "Are you actually going to advocate for me?"

"I didn't choose this role," his advocate said. "I would just as rather see you bound as anything."

He'd read about demons being bound before, trapped in a realm that wasn't life but wasn't death, either. The prospect shook him so much all he could say was, "Then fuck off." Bob gestured for him to go join the others on the far side of the ruined table. Gagthul shrugged and did so, allowing Bob to turn back to Olvauz. "What's the disaster here? I'm sorry for what happened to Xogmorech, but his fault was in getting caught and slain, not starting an entire city dancing."

"What of the others?" Olvauz asked. "They were all slain because of Xogmorch's plan."

"For decades, Aachen was off limits to our kind," the demon of teeth said.

"So what?" Bob started pacing. "Our duty is to tempt humans and take souls, is it not? If we can do that in the dozens or hundreds at one time, isn't that better than working one by one?"

"That is the problem. Not only do you have no idea of your wrong actions, you show no concern for the consequences of them," Olvauz said. "Remain here. The council will retire to deliberate on your fate."

Olvauz, the two other demons, the succubus, and the imp filed out of the room, the imp doing his best to keep up with his hop-step gait. Gagthul looked to Bob, shook his head, and followed them out.

Val and Bob were left alone, staring at each other across the broken table.

"I'm sorry," she said, after a long silence. "Olvauz said it would help you to know how this all happened."

Bob shrugged. "This is all just for show."

"I don't think so, Bob." She nodded toward the box on the floor.

It appeared to be a regular box, except for the writing on the outside that he couldn't understand.

"That's a prison," she said. "For our kind. Do you think they'd bring it here if they didn't intend to use it?"

"What?" He smiled.

"I can create a distraction," she said "you can get to the main gate and be gone. Give you a head start, at least. But you don't have much time!"

"Look, Val," he said, taking her face in his hands. "I appreciate what you're trying to do. But if I run, they'll know you helped and then you'll be in trouble. I couldn't leave you with that."

Before she could respond, the demons filed back in, this time with Olvauz bringing up the rear. He had a small book in one hand. Bob turned to face them. The succubus walked around behind Bob then positioned herself between Bob and Val. The demon of teeth went to his left, the demon without a mouth to his right.

"What's th..." Bob started to say, but Olvauz's booming voice cut him off.

"Hold him!"

The two demons each grabbed Bob by the arms, stopping any potential flight before it could begin. The succubus raised her hands to Val and snarled, but didn't need to actually make her back off.

"What?" Bob asked, focusing his attention on Olvauz. "What are you doing? "

Olvauz opened the box and held it one hand. "We are taking matters into our own hands. Our world exists in a kind of precarious balance with the world of the humans. We are more powerful beings, but there are so many more of them. Millions upon millions, more numerous than even the souls who languish in the realm of our master. If they are sufficiently motivated, they can end our kind."

"All the more reason to reap as many as we can at once!" Bob said. "You should envy me, use me as an example."

"For once, you are correct," Olvauz said. "You will certainly be an example." The book fell open in his other hand and he started reading, chanting in a strange guttural language.

Bob started to feel a heat rising inside his gut. It was like someone had reached inside him and lit a fire. It was spreading like a flood, up his chest and down into his legs, the internal fire racing to his fingertips. He howled in pain and would have fallen, if not for the two demons holding him up.

"Stop it!" Val screamed. "You can't slay one of our own!" She tried to take a step toward Olvauz, but the other succubus stopped her.

Olvauz kept reading, repeating the same stanza, over and over.

Bob felt the pain begin to subside, first in his feet, then in his lower legs. He quickly realized that was because they were vanishing, atomizing into their smallest parts, which were flowing into the box. "No! No! N..."

The box shut of its own accord. A flame danced across the seam between the lid and the body of the box, sealing it.

Val had her hands to her mouth, backing away.

Olvauz walked to her with the box. "Bobzolach has not been slain. There is nothingness after one of our kind is slain. It has little value as punishment. Binding, on the other hand, is a fate no demon wishes upon themselves."

"Can I...can I keep it?" She asked, voice cracking. "I don't want anything to happen to it. To him."

Olvauz shook his head. "No, Valgrelaath. Instead, you shall walk the Earth and tell the others of our kind what you have seen here, so they learn what happens to a tempter who would not think through the consequences of their actions. Do you understand?"

She nodded, slowly.

"Very well," Olvauz said. "This council's work is concluded. I suggest we all be gone by morning. The humans will be coming."

◇

The others drifted away, one by one, leaving Olvauz as the last one at the castle. Rather than follow, he remained overnight. When the sun had risen, he went back to the great hall. He put the box on the floor beside the ruined table. It pulsed with dark energy. He found a portion of the table that was almost flat and sat down, pulling his legs up underneath him and waited.

It wasn't long before the cardinal walked into the room.

"Are they still dancing?" Olvauz asked.

"It appears to be winding down, thank the Lord," the cardinal said. "Is it done?"

"It is," Olvauz said, without moving. "I hope it will be sufficient."

"The demon has been…punished?" the cardinal asked.

"In a more excruciating manner than your kind can imagine. Have you called off your parishioners? Is it safe for my kind to leave your jurisdiction?"

"Yes, yes." The cardinal's eyes drifted to the box on the floor. "Is that it?"

"It is," Olvauz said. "The one who set your city to dancing is interred there, for eternity. You, Cardinal, and everyone who ever carries the same title, will perish from this world, and he will still be stuck in that box."

"That seems appropriately demonic," the cardinal said, with a chuckle. "There is a spot on my mantle where it will go nicely."

"That seems appropriately human," Olvauz said, "taking joy in the failings of another."

The cardinal frowned. "Let us not part on such terms, Olvauz. I think we've come to a very satisfactory resolution to this whole mess. We can return to the way things should be."

"We need humans to tempt and souls to take. You need some threat to hold over your parishioners, an evil lurking around corners. If either side gets too successful, it throws the world out of balance." Olvauz chuckled. "The system works for both of us, doesn't it, your kind and mine?"

"Just as our creator needs your master for balance, so does the Church need your kind," the cardinal said. "The push and pull helps the people find their true, best selves."

"If that is what you tell yourself," Olvauz said. "Now, since you have what you demanded, shouldn't you be on your way?"

The cardinal stooped and picked up the box. "I hope you see I've been more than reasonable, Olvauz. Perhaps, sometime in the future, we can find another mutually advantageous arrangement?"

The fires of hell blazed in his eyes. "Let us hope not."

The cardinal left him without another word. Olvauz waited until he knew it was dark outside and crept to the main gate of the castle. He heard nothing aside from the buzzing of flies and rushing of the breeze. No voices. No clank of blades. No humans. The cardinal had kept his word.

Olvauz slipped out into the dark, back to a world that made some kind of sense. Even if he knew, deep in what the humans would have called his heart, that Bobzolach was right. Olvauz and the others were stuck in a safe, mutually beneficial relationship with the humans. It should be dangerous, it should be full of risk. It was time Olvauz remembered that he was a demon, first and foremost.

The Holy Harvest

Jocelyne Gregory

The Cathedral of Our Lady of Strasbourg was as grand as its name. It had taken four hundred years of construction to bring it to its present state, and it was the tallest cathedral Margaretta had ever seen in her young life.

After morning mass and before work pulled him away for the day, her father had often explained the reason for the angles, shapes and measurements of the carved stonework.

Sunlight pouring in through the stained-glass of the great rose window depicted the Last Judgement, the story of Adam and Eve and Noah's Ark. Her father had told her it was the history of the world, and it was important to know their place within that world.

"What happened, child?" Father Orleans sat beside Margaretta on the hard wooden bench. He had always been kind to her family. She knew he had employed her father when work was scarce, and visited her aging grandmother who could no longer make the long walk for communion.

"Is she mute? How old is she?"

Margaretta glanced at the speaker and immediately cast her gaze to the stone floor when she met hardened brown eyes. He arrived a day earlier with two other men demanding to speak with her about what she had witnessed that summer.

"My Lord Ricci, she can speak. She is just scared. This will be her thirteenth summer," Father Orleans soothed.

"Record that, Brother Lucius," Lord Ricci ordered. He wore jewelled rings on each finger, and fashionably rich clothing with a fine starched collar at his throat.

"*Si*, lord," Brother Lucius mumbled. He clutched his brown traveler's cloak tight with one hand. He resembled a monk with his long robes and a woolen cap to keep his head warm. He sat beside the benches with a small table and several pages of fresh parchment. With his ink-stained fingertips and quill, he recorded every word and gesture of the meeting.

Margaretta noticed the last man of the group said nothing. Instead, he leaned against the benches with his gaze trained on the figures of Adam and Eve. He wore all black, with no cap to cover his thinning hair, or starched collar at his throat.

"Child, can you tell us what happened in the summer? Do not fear, you have done no wrong, and you will not be punished. You are only here to tell the lawyers of the Holy Mother Church what you witnessed," Father Orleans explained.

"Y—Yes, Father," Margaretta said. She looked down to her hands and fidgeted with her mother's old worn rosary. She was silent for a few minutes before she spoke. "It started with the night sky."

"The sky?" Lord Ricci asked.

"Yes, lord," Margaretta said. "It was a hot summer's night. I could not sleep in my room with my two sisters, so I went outside with our dog and a blanket. There was a faint breeze, but I found a spot on the grass to sleep on. There were others like me that night, I think. I was falling asleep when I saw this streak in the sky, like a candle flame flying through the night."

"Make note of the flying," Lord Ricci murmured to Brother Lucius.

"What happened to the flame?" Father Orleans asked.

"It flew through the sky." Margaretta raised her hands and repeated the motion she had watched. "It flew left, and it flew right. I thought it was an angel dancing in the heavens," she confessed.

"Did this angel appear before you?" Lord Ricci asked.

"No, lord." Margaretta shook her head. "It flew around for a while before it crashed into the river. It was so loud I could hear the splash."

"Do you remember this, Father?" Lord Ricci tilted his head.

"I admit I was asleep," Father Orleans explained. "I do remember that night being very hot though. I ordered the doors to the cathedral opened wide to allow for the breeze off the river, and many people came that night and slept here on the cool floor."

"What happened next, child?" Lord Ricci focused on Margaretta.

"The next day, I saw Frau Troffea gathering water from the river. Oh, it was so hot. I was on my way to deliver some ale for my uncle. She offered me some, and I declined."

"Ale?" Lord Ricci frowned.

"Her family runs a brewery," Father Orleans said. "Her father was deeply involved in helping the church, and the family is faithfully devout."

Margaretta glanced at him. It seemed odd to her how forceful his voice sounded.

"Good." Lord Ricci seemed to relax at Father Orleans' words. "This Frau Troffea drank the water from the river, and when she offered you some, you refused?"

"Yes, lord. Father said to only drink boiled water."

"Carry on."

"It wasn't soon after that she began to dance." Margaretta's brows tugged together, and she absently rolled her mother's rosary between her fingers. "She danced like we do when we finish the autumn harvest and thank God for his bounty. She danced like someone was hitting a drum and was making music for her, but I couldn't hear anything."

"A witches' sabbath?" Lord Ricci gasped.

Brother Lucius gasped and quickly made the sign of the cross which Lord Ricci repeated. Father Orleans did the same and Margaretta did as well. She noted that the quiet man did not move, but he seemed more interested in her words.

"Girl, did you see the witches' sabbath?" Lord Ricci leaned closer to her.

"N—no, lord." Margaretta swallowed hard. "At least I don't think so?"

"Is this Frau Troffea Christian?" He asked Father Orleans.

"She is, lord. I checked the records myself. The only time she has missed mass was during the summer months," Father Orleans explained.

"I see. Continue." Lord Ricci sat back on the bench.

Margaretta pushed her worries down and squeezed her mother's rosary hard in the palm of her hand. She took a deep breath and continued. "Soon, other women joined her and began to dance with her. Father and Mother said I was to stay away from her, that she might be sick, so I did as they said. But Father…" her words trailed off.

"Your father?" Lord Ricci asked.

"Yes, Frau Troffea's father came to my father one night and begged his help to take her home. He thought she was possessed, and she wasn't eating anything but drank only river water. Father agreed to help him. He said it was the good Christian thing to do, to help those who needed help as our Lord Jesus did." Margaretta's voice cracked. "So, he left, and when he didn't come home the next morning, Mother went to find him."

Margaretta fell quiet as tears rolled down her cheeks. She quickly brushed them away and clenched her mother's rosary tight. "S—She did not come back that night. I took my younger sisters and brought them to my grandmother for safety. And—and I went to get my parents."

"And where were they, child?" Lord Ricci asked.

"They were dancing," Margaretta confessed. "I ran to them. I grabbed their hands and arms." She grabbed at the air. "And I tried to drag them away, but they would not stop dancing. I saw Father Orleans trying to drag people away too, but they wouldn't stop dancing, and some became violent!"

"It's true, but I do not blame them. They could not control themselves in their state," Father Orleans said.

"This was early in the summer?" Lord Ricci frowned.

"Yes, lord. Nobody would stop. Those that did only stopped because they fell to the ground dead. I could not let that happen to my parents." Margaretta wiped the tears from her cheeks. "They would not eat or drink our ale, so I brought them river water and they drank that for days and weeks, until..." She bit her bottom lip.

"Until?" Lord Ricci said.

"Father, should I?" Margaretta looked to Father Orleans.

"Yes, child," he said. He took her hands in his and squeezed them tight.

"What is it?" Lord Ricci's frown deepened.

Margaretta opened her mouth and closed it. Her lips soured and she shifted uneasy on the bench. She looked towards the stained-glass windows and sent a silent prayer to the heavens before she whispered the words, "The angels appeared."

Brother Lucius' quill snapped. He muttered beneath his breath as he hurriedly opened a box on the table and brought out a replacement. He dipped it in ink and quickly wrote down what she had just uttered.

"Angels?" The quiet man asked.

"Yes, the angels," she said.

"Tell us about these angels. What did they say, what did they look like, did they have wings?" Lord Ricci demanded.

"They were of light," Margaretta whispered. She kept her eyes on the stained-glass window as she spoke. "It was almost night, and the sun was beginning to set. Mother and Father and all the dancers, they looked like skeletons from lack of food, and they were drenched in sweat, and their gazes were directed towards the sky. But suddenly they all reached towards it, like this." Margaretta raised her hands above her head like she was reaching for the great ceiling of the cathedral. "And the angels came down, like solid white mist, and enveloped one dancer after the other." She lowered her arms and rested her hands on her lap.

"An embrace?" Lord Ricci murmured.

"I think so, lord," Margaretta said. "The angels, and there were many of them, they embraced the dancers and took this glittering light from each person's body into their own white mist. When the angels finished their embrace, the dancer's dropped to the ground exhausted or..."

"Or?"

"Or dead," Margaretta whispered. "It was like the angels were taking their souls from their bodies to bring to God."

"How long did the angels' visitation last?" Lord Ricci asked.

"All night," she said. "I watched from nearby. I was scared. The angels did not speak or if they did, I could not hear them. They had no wings, but they floated from one person to the next. And when the sun set, they glowed like lights in the dark night. It wasn't until the sun rose and the last dancer collapsed to the ground did the angels drift back up to the heavens."

"Those that survived, we brought into the church and took care of as best we could. Those who passed, we buried with prayers," Father Orleans said.

"I see," Lord Ricci said. He looked to the scribe beside him. "End it there."

Brother Lucius bowed his head and put his quill down.

"Girl, why do you think you were spared the angels' embrace when so many others were afflicted?" Lord Ricci tilted his head, and his eyes focused on Margaretta.

"I do not know, Lord," Margaretta confessed. "Father Orleans said it was God's will that I was spared, and I know that I shall see my mother and father in the kingdom of heaven one day. I just wish they had not been taken so soon. I, and my sisters, miss them very much."

"Do not weep. They are with him, and they watch over you now and always until you join them when God deems it time," Father Orleans comforted.

Margaretta sniffled and wiped her eyes once more. "Thank you, Father. May I go now? I need to get home to my sisters and grandmother. She is not well."

"One last question, child," Lord Ricci said. "Have you any strange dreams or visions of the white angels since you saw them? Have you dreamed of your parents since their passing?"

Margaretta frowned at his words. "I don't think so. Wait, I have!" She gasped in realization. "I had a dream just last night. I saw mother and father outside the front door. They were wiggling on their bellies like worms after a storm, but different."

"Worms? Are you certain? Not parasites?" The quiet man asked.

"It is strange, lord. Now that I think of it, they were like both. They coiled like parasites on their sides as though they were full of energy. I know because my dog has coughed up similar things in the past when he was sick," Margaretta said.

"Thank you, Margaretta," Lord Ricci said. He reached for his coin purse and pulled it free. He offered the heavy bag to her. "This is for you."

"Lord!" Margaretta's mouth fell open. "I—I cannot."

Lord Ricci took her hand in his and placed the coin purse in her grasp. "You must. You have suffered, but you have also faithfully given testimony to the Mother Church. Use this money to help take care of your sisters, your grandmother, and yourself. But you must never speak of our meeting, except only to Father Orleans, do you understand?"

"Y—Yes, lord. Oh, thank you, lord. Thank you," Margaretta rambled. She hugged the purse tight to her chest. She watched as Lord Ricci, Brother Lucius, and the quiet man stood and left the cathedral without another word. She turned to Father Orleans when they were gone. "What has happened? Why did they leave?"

"You have done well, Margaretta," Father Orleans whispered. "Brother Lucius and Lord Ricci are satisfied with your testimony. I was worried the other one would demand more."

"The quiet man? Who is he?"

"He is the witch hunter of the Holy Mother Church, Margaretta. If he had not believed your words, your sisters and your grandmother would be burned at the stake alongside you," he explained.

"But I didn't do anything wrong." Margaretta gasped.

Father Orleans shook his head. "It matters not. Your parents were afflicted by the dance, and you were near them. It is by God's grace you were spared twice from the dance and the witch hunter's gaze. Come, let me walk you home. You must keep that money safe."

"Yes, Father Orleans. Thank you."

Margaretta and Father Orleans left the grand cathedral together. She clutched the purse and held it close to her heart. Her sisters and grandmother would eat well that night, and when everyone had gone to bed, she would pray that she could dream of her parents once more.

The Third Ministration

C. Owen Loftus

J went to the cathedral to ask for a new name. I'd just stolen most of a text, see, in which Chalcidius speaks glowingly of the physician Alcmaeon of Croton, and I realized that if I was ever going to be seen as their equal, I needed to take a page out of their book. I showed that page to Father Aragon. After squinting at it and reading the text by moving his lips, he made a sound of demurring and shrugged. Even after I escorted him across the library to the shelves with the baptismal records and waited with an ungodly amount of patience for him to thumb through the pages of his own smeared handwriting to find my entry, he only licked his lips and blinked wetly at me.

"Father," I said, "let's get on with it." I dipped a quill and brandished it at him, hoping the aggression would surprise him into taking it from my hand.

Instead, he tried to say something, but choked on the motion in his throat. After an agonizing heartbeat of gagging, he spit out the lump with just enough force to clear his lips. The thick yellow snot dripped down his chin, and I put a little distance between us for the sake of my shirt.

I shouted out the door, "Is anyone else here?" and watched Aragon in case he decided to drop dead on the floor. He actually did look a little like he might collapse, so I aimed him at a chair and nudged until he fell into it. His head drooped and he stared through the space between his knees. His jowls worked like he was still trying to read that page. Alcmaeon Alcmaeon Alcmaeon Alcmaeon Alcmaeon Alcmaeon Chalcidius.

Someone did come eventually. This new priest was fat and balding. A fresh scar split his lower lip into two dangling lumps of flesh. He told me that the only thing more batshit than Father Aragon was my stupid reason for bothering him. I disagreed, but perhaps I did so with too much vehemence, because I was soon flanked by two acolytes with faces almost as ugly. One grabbed my shoulders, the other swept my feet, and before I could react, I was dangling between them like so much educated jerky.

Still, before they marched me out the building like a Muslim out of Jerusalem, I had to ask what was wrong with Aragon.

"I'm a doctor," I said. "A good one. I can help."

"He's just old," Three Lips said through his mangled mouth. "Hopefully he'll die soon so you can't bother him."

They deposited me *au gratin* onto a pile of food scraps rotting in the gutter, just underneath Aragon's window. I watched the light from his fire turn the sill gold in the blueing dusk and considered what Three Lips had said. He was old, that was true. Much older than he'd been the last time I'd seen him, even accounting for the years in between. I crossed myself for his sake, then piled some spoiled potatoes into a tiny shrine for passing faeries, just in case. I had to promise Dionysus I'd make it up to him later.

◇

I keep my promises, so the next day dawned for me in the late afternoon. I stumbled onto the busy street, swore at the sun for taking up the gauntlet with me and set out to find some food. My rented room was cheap, and the food my landlords offered was best avoided.

I finally found someone willing to trade a bowl of stew for some bloodletting. I blew on it as I walked and let myself become slightly lost. I'd been away long enough that the streets felt unfamiliar and riddled with opportunity. It matched my thoughts. My time in Pembroke had been enlightening, but strange. Maybe I'd let the pagans' superstitions bore too many holes in me. My head was honeycombed. So, I relished the fresh certainty of my birthplace and the symbolic freedom of losing myself inside it.

Still, I knew the neighborhood, so when nursing my hair-ache became more important than eating, I found my way home without too much trouble.

I turned the last corner and found my door blocked by a crowd that milled around a woman who wiggled her arms in a tired way. I tapped the nearest man's shoulder and asked why everyone found this so interesting.

"She's been dancing all day," he whispered.

"Oh," I said, "I can sort of see that's dancing."

He shook his head.

"No, I mean all she does is dance. I've been watching her since sunup, and she hasn't stopped for anything."

"Busy day for you, huh?"

The man scowled and turned back to the show.

The woman was dirty enough for it to be true. It also bought her some charity for how little grace she showed in her form. But it was hot, as hot as it gets all year, and I could tell her blood was boiling even from this distance. She was lucky not to have dropped from exhaustion.

I tapped the stranger again, and even though he pretended to ignore me, I could tell he noticed from the way he darted his eyes.

"Why is she dancing?" I asked.

He answered, though he looked as if I'd pinched him.

"She doesn't know. We've been trying to get her to stop, but she just keeps going."

"Help, please," she said. Her lips were so dry and cracked that they bled from the talking. She hung her head and let her jaw quiver in a pose of unthinking supplication, and for a moment I saw Father Aragon superimposed on her face.

I pushed my way to the door, climbed the stairs and watched from my window while I changed into relatively clean clothes. Someone held a cup of water to the girl's mouth. She sipped it but continued with her jerky wobbling.

She was still there the next morning, though it was early, and the street was nearly deserted. She must not be a beggar, then, just another stranger giving up to the heat. I avoided looking at her.

I plied my trade all that day. I'm good at finding custom, but any doctor could here. The city was full of buboes and fevers and infertile young women trading gold coins for potions.

A man approached me while I washed vomit off my tools at a public fountain.

"Hello," he said. He cleared his throat nervously, and said again, "Hello."

I met his eyes briefly without turning my head. My knives are sharp.

"Hello," I said. "Can I do something for you?"

He blushed and stammered a little.

"Do you remember me?" I did, once he asked. He was the one who I'd spoken with about the dancing girl. He looked at the clean instruments I'd spread out to dry on the lip of the fountain's bowl and spoke again before I could answer. "Are you a doctor?"

"Yes. A good one." The pause was perfect, and I nearly shivered at the effect. A doctor gets custom by saying things dramatically.

"Will you come to help?" he asked. He was frightened, and it sobered me.

"Yes," I said, and began to gather my things. "Where are we going?"

"Bentham Street." When I stood, he moved into the crowd, then stopped, and turned to see if I was coming. I was, but I nearly had to skip to match his stride. The man was huge, at least a full head taller than me. I followed him, and he led me home.

◇

The crowd was much bigger now. At its center were six women, linked at the elbow in pairs, twirling over a puddle of their own piss and shit.

When does a sore become a sickness? As I watched, another teen stepped into the circle and began to spin, arm aloft as if held by an invisible partner. Whatever started here was spreading. To stop it, I had to get closer. But my frame tends towards the slight, and there were seven of them. My eyes settled on the bulk of the man who brought me.

"Are you brave?" I asked him.

He showed the whites of his eyes, but he nodded.

"Good. What's your name?"

"Vauqelin," he said.

"Good enough."

Then I took his elbow and pulled him with me into the dance.

People laughed, but that changed to jeers when I turned Vauqelin's enormous body into the way of an oncoming couple.

I expected at least one of them to halt at the intrusion, but neither did. They spun right into him and bounced off his chest. Once off balance they fell into the muck. Even on their sides they kept their grip on each other and ran their legs like spinning wheels. Vauqelin proved himself immediately. Instead of pulling away from the splatter of offal, he dropped to one knee and pulled the girls up by their armpits. They resumed their twirling, but stayed in more or less the same spot after that.

I stood as close as I could to their circle, watching each of their faces in turn as they passed. One was a waif-thin girl, maybe twelve. She stared at me with wild eyes. The other was a woman with matted brown hair and a pointed jaw – the first dancer. She smiled at me out of one corner of her mouth, and I decided this was the place to start.

"My name is Arthurius Rex Apollyon Peter of Golgotha," I said. "I am a physician, tutored in Rome and the hill lands of Wales. I am here to help."

"Fantastic," the woman said. She was interrupted by her dancing taking her the other way. "If you would do something, that would be great."

"This," I said, "is my man, Vitus, named for the holy man who is his guide. Some claim he is the saint incarnate, sent to heal us in these troubled times."

He blanched and blushed at the same time, which I assumed was unhealthy.

"Hi," said the woman. "Sorry." A spin. "I'd greet you formally." Spin. "But I can't." Spin. "I'm dancing, see."

"Why?" I asked.

"Good question." Spin. "You're the doctor." Spin. "Are you any good?"

"Very good," Vauqelin said. The smile I flashed at him was genuine.

Turning back, I asked, "What's your name?"

"Mel. There's more, but..." Spin. "Well."

"Yes," I said. "Mel, would it be all right if we begin?"

"Please," she said. "I'm tired as a pope saving prostitutes."

◇

I tried restraining her first, of course. She just wiggled around on the ground. I told Vauqelin to let her up when her heels started bleeding from knocking against the cobblestones.

Then we turned to herbs. I had a few basics on my person, and willing couriers in the crowd to find anything else I needed. It all worked as expected; the emetics kicked her bile upstream, and the diarrhetics kicked it down river. But there was little change to her condition. Over the hours I made her phlegmatic, sanguine, and choleric in turn. In a desperate move to beat the fading light, I mixed her a noxious tea with everything I had left to make her the most melancholic she'd ever be without catching on fire. Still, the only thing we accomplished was adding to the pile of excrement under her feet.

As night fell, I packed my things and ordered Vauqelin to lead the remaining onlookers in thirty-three Hail Marys. It was unscientific, but it couldn't hurt. Doctors get custom when they show a little piety. That, and I hoped the token effort would exorcize the almost-ghost of Father Aragon from the back of my head.

I needed to think. I was stymied, and a little baffled. Delayed success infuriated me. I'd never encountered a problem I couldn't dissolve in a tincture. I just had to find the right one.

In my room, in a locked chest tucked inside the foot of my straw tick, were my books. I pulled them out and read them all again, one by one. The gold-painted names on their covers sparkled in the candlelight.

It took all night, but I finally found what I was looking for in a volume bound in white calfskin. I slid a page of Chalcidius in it to mark my place and blew out the candles.

In the quiet of my solved problem, I heard Vauqelin snoring. How long had he been there? He must have followed me inside, uninvited, and fallen asleep on the floor. I snorted through my nose, but it wasn't worth doing anything about now. My guts were aching to get into bed. I dropped the pillow near Vauqelin's head and covered myself head to toe in the rough blanket. Soon I was asleep, and rapidly turning the pages of a book, written in Gaelic, that disappeared the moment I read the words.

◇

We split a loaf of moldy rye bread the next morning in the doorway of my house. The dancers, Mel included, were stomping and clapping today, albeit without any particular rhythm. The landlady brought us some pallid wine that I spit out after a sip, but Vauqelin swallowed the skin in one draft. It made him want to talk, so I let him while I picked the bugs from between my teeth that the bread had left behind.

His surname was Troffea, and he'd been a cavalier of moderately noble blood until he'd failed so abysmally in the war with Italy that his family sent him away in embarrassment. I was surprised he was willing to share the story. The man must be exceptionally lonely.

"Killing is easy," I told him. "It's a waste of talent. Saving lives is a much better use of your time." Then I gave him some instructions on how to begin the day's treatment. I'd join him, I said, as soon as I could. Then I went back to the cathedral.

I found Aragon in his quarters, tied to a chair next to the window. Seeing it made me hot behind the eyes. I used my surgery knife to cut the rope and without hesitation he fell on his face. I lunged to catch him and tried to prop him back up, but his back was limp. He didn't react to me through it all. His eyes followed the square of sky.

Then, I understood. He wanted the light but couldn't support himself upright. Someone put him in the chair and made sure he wouldn't fall out. I looked around for another idea, sighed, and replaced his supports, gently as I could.

When I was finished, he smiled at the warmth on his face. His shoulders relaxed into the thin padding. Then, like before, his mouth began to waggle.

"What are you trying to say?" I asked, but I didn't expect an answer. He followed the birds flitting over the street with his eyes, and soon began to doze.

"Wake up," I said. "There's so much we need to talk about."

But he didn't wake up, so I padded out of the chamber and closed the door.

Three Lips was in the hallway; he spat on the ground when he saw me.

"I'm leaving," I said.

"Good," he said. "Don't come back."

When I passed him, I kicked backwards into the soft part behind his knee. He lost his balance, and from the sound of it fell right into a candelabra. I didn't look to see. A doctor doesn't get custom by demeaning himself.

◇

I began the day's work by preparing Mel's humours with bloodletting. Vauqelin pincered one arm to the ground, and I made the cuts with the same blade that untied Aragon.

"That's a lot of blood," Vauqelin said.

"We're doing a whole day's worth at once," I said. "I don't want to have to hold her down again." I opened another vein, and her free arm swung up and smacked me in the throat. I drowned out her apology with my swearing in Latin. "God dammit. Whenever we steady one part of her, the rest just gets worse."

"It's a horrid equilibrium," Mel said in the same language. I raised an eyebrow.

"Where did you learn that?" I asked.

"*I ligere*," she said. I read. Then she smashed her face against the street and broke her nose.

When her body was ready, I began to work in earnest. Her blood was hot, and I was going to cool it. I knew it with a certainty that lit sparks on my breath bright enough to light a solstice fire.

Bentham Street turned to bedlam around me. Artists and prophets and pickpockets swarmed like wide-eyed locusts out of some banal level of hell to nibble at my fingers. Soldiers and politicians and lesser breeds of alchemists tried to latch on and parasitize the glory that would inevitably come. I paid it all no mind. My work was demanding at the best of times, and a doctor gets custom from their ability to focus.

I squeezed blood from hunks of flesh peeled out of butchers' shops, and dipped chafing fingers into stinging powders buried deep in apothecary cabinets. I burned all manner of unspeakable things and blew the smoke into Mel's face. It irritated her eyes and made the irises all the more green.

But when night came, Mel still paroxysmed away. Her expression was apologetic, but her body writhed in joy. Her unblooded cheeks shone like opal in the moonlight. It made me so choleric I saw spots.

I was failing, and in front of the entire city. I screamed wordlessly from the back of my throat and left the dancers' circle, kicking anyone who stood in my path. Vauqelin caught up to me shortly, toting my things in his arms. When he tried to talk, I screamed again and kicked a wall.

When we made it back to my room, my shoe was full of blood. I'd torn off a nail. I threw it into the pile with the other gored things I'd ruined this week and threw myself into bed. I shrieked hoarsely into the tick until my voice left me.

◇

When I was sure Vauqelin was asleep, I put on my blood-soaked boots.

The door to the street was blocked by the sagging silhouette of my landlady. She pressed hot loaves of bread into my hands and kissed my cheek.

"For your godliness in helping those afflicted by the daemons," she said.

I took them but said nothing. My throat hurt.

◇

By the time I reached the cathedral, I was fully awake and angry in a way that made the dark streets vibrate. I found an unlocked door near the kitchen and groped my way to Aragon's chamber. He was in bed, thanks to God. I set the loaves on a table where I was sure he'd find them. As I left, I heard him whisper, "Thank you."

"Of course, Father," I said. Then I shut the door and jogged down the hallway. I had no coin to spend on men who were already dead.

I found the library and began tearing books off the shelves. Histories, histories, nothing but histories. Finally, in the corner behind the church records, I found both a grimoire and a pharmacopeia. I stepped on the editions I'd thrown on the floor to settle into a chair. The illustrations were perfect. The ink was vivid against the cream sheafs. I didn't need a light to see them. The print was so sharp it cut the pads of my fingers.

The vermin found me eventually, of course. The priests nickered and lowed and introduced me to councilmen who forced things to read into my pockets, but I ignored them until I learned what I needed. Once I did, I tucked the books under my armpit, damned all the clergy for hindering a doctor's healing work, and left for Bentham Street. I didn't have the patience for groveling little lackwits biting at the nape of my neck, making their intolerable noises.

I had a cure, despite the interruptions. My mistake had been relying on the decaying knowledge of dead men. This dancing was a new thing entirely and needed a treatment as alive as we were, as alive as the woods around Pembroke under the moon before All Saints' Day. I strode home, and the street shook in time to the pounding of faraway pagans' feet.

I returned to find Vauqelin performing as instructed. I nodded in greeting without stopping, seized Mel by the face, and probed the soft parts of her head, testing, looking.

I palpated all the dancers, now a dozen strong. Their feet were bleeding, their joints were swollen, their throats were dry, their eyes inflamed, their bowels loose, their hair falling out. They cried in the agony of exposed flesh with every step in the rhythm I now recognized and remembered.

When I was done looking, I began curing. I cut, and soaked, and tapped, and bent and cursed them all as bastards even though I could barely talk. The things I demanded Vauqelin fetch me grew increasingly strange and poisonous.

It didn't work, but I was almost there. I knew it. I was sure. And though I stopped for half a blink's length because I couldn't justify my knowing it, part of the sureness was knowing that sort of thing didn't matter anymore. Tonight would be the last night we were haunted. I wiped my bloody hands on the thighs of my pants and gestured to Vauqelin to come over.

"I need two things. First, torches. Second, I need my books. Bring them here and then find more."

He chewed his lower lip.

"Maybe you should rest. There's a–"

I stopped him.

"I need two things," I said, and repeated the instructions, word for word, just as I'd written them in my head.

This time, he agreed, and soon was gone.

I tried to address the crowd of onlookers, but it made me cough until I spat up blood from my raw throat. I swore at myself for sending Vauqelin away, then cornered one of the hermits preaching from the gutter and had him repeat my hoarse whispers at a volume everyone could hear.

"I need space," my proxy said for me. "Leave Bentham Street. You can watch from the intersections if you like."

The crowd booed. I waited a moment for the swell of noise to crest.

"That, or expose yourselves to the new plague."

That last word was enough. Like any city, like every city, this one was still afraid. By the time the moon peeked over the rooftops, I was alone with the crying dancers, and my sureness. I'd identified the sickness, which meant I was a hair's breadth from the cure.

The veins in my fingers pulsed to music I couldn't hear but knew by heart. My temples throbbed at the echoes of shouts I'd unknowingly carried inside me from a distant country to the nursery of my original sin. My nerves popped like living flesh in sacrificial flames.

In retaliation, the secret anger I kept in my bag of things broke the clasps and poured into Bentham Street, immersing the dancers, myself, and all.

Once encompassed, I was subsumed and could begin the true communion. I sat where I stood. The stink of the street soaked into my clothes and pooled in the wrinkles of my skin. The stain turned the covers of my lovely books brown between the gold, so I plucked them like sunflowers from their muddy fields and ate them, one by one. Their seeds sprouted in my belly and grew through my veins until the leaves poked out from behind my eyes.

The next dawn was a meaty pink. It woke me from a fitful doze, and without thinking I left my reading and walked to the corner to stretch my back and watch the sky blush. When it changed to blue, I turned back, and saw Mel sitting on a stoop rubbing her calves.

"You've stopped," I gasped.

"Yup. Janine did first, and then we all just...stopped."

The others were spread across the damp street, leaning against walls and gingerly cleaning their feet. My throat tightened, and I was forced to choose my words carefully.

"Why?" I asked.

"I dunno." She grabbed her elbows and held herself against a cool breeze. "It's hard to remember clearly. I've been pretty stressed out. Maybe it was something you did?"

"No," I said. "I wasn't finished yet."

The silence where the slapping meat of her dancing had been hurt my ears.

"Did you ever figure out why we started?" she asked.

"No," I said.

It hurt so bad. Silence couldn't hurt, could it?

"You did your best. I'm lucky to have had you as my very good doctor."

"No," I said.

That was what hurt. It was the way the names on the spines of my books reflected the light and blinded me.

Mel turned petulant.

"I won't compliment you if you don't appreciate it. Really, you worked so hard–"

"No," I said. Why was that all I could say?

"Yes," Mel said. "Hippocrates himself would–"

"*No.*" I tried to scream, but my voice was ruined, and my anger was turned to salt. I tried to stir what rage remained pooled in the gutter but found its flesh cold and dead.

"Sorry," Mel said. "Holy Father's vestments, Arthur, calm down. This is supposed to be good news."

When I didn't answer, she left my side and laid down with a poorly transcribed copy of Paracelsus for a pillow. She was asleep in an instant.

All of them were. I watched them dream while I tried to take stock. The last few days weren't very clear for me either.

I returned to my piles of books. Sometime in the night I'd stacked them in a circle around my spot in the gutter, though I didn't remember doing so. Many of them were rare, most were handsome, and all were ruined. The lowest in each stack was swollen with sewage, and when I riffled through the nearest every page was discolored by foul brown fingerprints.

In the chill left behind by my anger's death, I felt my senses return to me. I smelt like a plague house and looked like a cemetery. Other people's blood coated every exposed part of me. Their vomit flecked my beard. My clothes were unsalvageable, stiff as they were with pressed bile and fever sweat. My knives and saws were covered in slime and rusting. Many lay pressed into the mire by the dancers' bare feet, undoubtedly ruined by the rot soaking into their wood handles.

I wouldn't be able to replace any of it, either. Doctors dipped in shit get very little custom. But even after a bath, no one would ever hire me. I couldn't imagine a more public way to expose my incompetence.

I began the slow process of gathering what was scattered across Bentham Street. The crowd ogled me from around the corner. Their eyes were insatiable. The quarantine line still held, but who knew for how long. How best, I wondered, to enjoy your last few minutes as a doctor, even a poor one?

I dropped the knives into their satchel. They fell on an unfamiliar sheaf of papers. I pulled them out, did my best to wipe off the muck and recognized them as what I'd been handed in the library at the cathedral. I must have stuffed them in my bag during my rush to leave.

It was a letter, a long one, from the magistrate. I read it, rubbed my chin and then read it again. I read it six more times, then made up my mind.

One by one I roused the sleeping afflicted. We spoke quietly, and when I left them, they began, again, to dance.

Mel was the last.

"Wake up," I said, and she smiled when she saw my face.

"Arthur. Why are you in my bed?"

"I want you to read this." I showed her the letter, but rather than take it she scowled and covered her eyes with her forearm.

"I'm too tired," she said. "You read it."

"It's money, Mel. So much money. The crown wants to pay me whatever I need to cure the Dancing Plague."

"But we did that already," she said.

"Yes. But right now, no one else knows that."

She frowned crossly, but her expression changed when she saw the other girls dancing across the cobblestones.

"They all agreed?" she asked, bewildered.

"Yes."

She thought for a moment and then took the papers.

"How much money?"

◇

We danced for weeks on the magistrate's gold.

When someone's exhaustion overcame their greed, I nursed them back to health. In exchange, they told the city about my kindness, my genius, the necessity of me and only me retaining total control over the plague. We replaced them by making whispered promises to select desperate people in taverns, where it was too crowded to overhear a conversation.

The strange internal consistency of my inexplicable and singular relevance lent me an air of unapproachable talent. I was invited to medical schools to teach, and churches to sermonize and manors to fall in love with rich daughters. Soon I had dozens of important people vying for my time and a hundred dancers for them to gape at from a safe distance.

The deception rested on my reputation. I cured dancers every day; publicly if I could manage it, surrounded by screaming onlookers. But I made sure more fell ill to keep the city grateful.

My fame rose, and my afflicted horde grew by the gross. They spilled across the streets without thought or obstacle. The miasma of fear grew so overwhelming that by the end, I could just tell someone they needed to dance, and they'd begin. Who were they to argue? The name Arthurius Rex was spoken over every pulpit during Sunday Mass.

The only ones who died were people who came of their own accord. I think most of them joined as a joke and simply got overwhelmed by the heat. Three weeks in, I dealt with a migration of particularly suicidal zealots that I attributed to the variety dancing offered to their daemons, who must have needed a change of pace from the flagellating. But a few carried a smell of honest panic on them that occupied my thoughts at night. I'd crafted the plague, but those last ones made me certain I'd also discovered a disease. When this was finished, and I had the time, I'd heal them. First, I'd visit Father Aragon, and then I'd go be a doctor again.

It was Mel's idea to build the stage.

"Play me some music so I feel less stupid," she said, and although I knew she was kidding it struck me. Maybe I could salve my conscience by spending just a little of my stolen power on something beautiful. We built a floor for the dancers to traipse across, then hired musicians of every sort.

Mel made them all play at the same time. It was a cacophony fit for the stinking hordes who chose to dance here instead of killing themselves with whatever they'd been using before.

She laughed until she puked, and Vauqelin blushed while he held her hair. I just felt cold.

Being Vitus was his adventure. He bought a horse and talked sometimes about riding it back to his family home, though I was never sure if he intended to mend bridges or rub his money in their faces. Mel blossomed as the Lady Melende, the daughter of a suddenly and massively successful grain merchant. He bought half the available property in town and slathered her in dresses, between her recurring bouts with the plague.

Imagine, then, the amounts of money that must have been involved when her father accepted Vitus' proposal of marriage without even a counteroffer on the dowry.

◇

The day before the wedding, she feigned a collapse and called me to her sick bed. Her new address was prestigious. The house was large, and the walls were covered in tapestries. A servant answered the door when I knocked, and I found Mel drowning in an enormous pile of goose down and silk.

"I'm not going back out," she said. "I got everything I wanted."

I rubbed my eyes with the heels of my palms.

"True," I said, "But did your father? Or Vauqelin?"

"Vitus," she corrected, and laughed in a way that reminded me of Pembroke. It was no wonder he'd fallen in love with her.

"It won't last," I said, and she frowned. Shadows caught in the lines it etched around her mouth.

"Are you threatening me?" she said.

"Not by intention. I only meant that our income relies on reciprocity."

"I'll be fine, thanks." She flared her nostrils, clenched her jaw, then said, "Please go."

I picked up my hat, headed for the door and changed my mind. I turned back to face Mel. I wanted to see her eyes.

"Marry me instead," I said.

The pity that flushed over her face made me nauseous.

"He's a stupid soldier who lost his name. I'm a doctor, a good one. I can provide for you in ways he never will."

Her lips parted, then pressed together.

"He's a good man," she said. "I love him."

"Please," I said. I hated myself in that moment, but then I started to hate her, because the revulsion I felt was suddenly in her eyes too.

She licked her lips, and said, "I'm sorry."

I crossed her room in one stride and punched her in the jaw.

She began to cry. I didn't know what to do. I knelt and clutched her to my chest while her body wracked with sobs. I tried to wipe her tears with my hands, but I left smeared tracks of blood behind my split knuckles.

"I'm telling everyone," she whispered through hiccups.

"What?" I said, and held her at arm's length.

"Everyone," she said. "Everything."

I ran from the room like a dog after thunder.

The streets vibrated again for the first time since the plague died, this time in wild shakes that threw me against the building walls. But I made it to my room and prepared the mixture quickly. I put it in a vial that I held in front of me while I ran the miles back. I was going too fast, I couldn't see or hear or stop, and when I knocked on the door, I couldn't tell if someone answered until the medicine was plucked from my fingers.

"Mel has to drink this tea now, right now, in this very moment, or everything is lost." I gasped for the air I'd used to talk. The servant kissed me and spoke softly in my ear.

"How can we thank you, Doctor?" she said. "You're a godly soul to care for others when you can barely stand up yourself."

"Yes," I said. "My work is hard and cruel."

I ran away again, until I tripped on a loose cobblestone and fell over a waist-high fence into a little garden. I lay in the dirt until the Frau found me there, nearly blind and deaf, dancing like a Celt in Cemais under the growing vegetables.

◇

By the time I was sensate enough to make my way to the cathedral, Vauqelin had stationed soldiers at the door. I was forced to wait until dark and then clamber through a window. I stumbled to Father Aragon's chamber and found him asleep inside. Three Lips sat in the chair by the fire and didn't seem surprised to see me.

"Come for your last confession?" he said.

I checked the corners of the room. The three of us were alone.

"I'll hear it," he said, "but the guards have to know you're here afterwards."

"Not you," I said. "Him." I nodded at Aragon's shivering silhouette.

"No," Three Lips said. "He's dying. Let him do it in peace."

"I have to talk to him," I said, and it made Three Lips mournful.

"Do you think he wants to see you like this?" he asked. "His last memory of you shouldn't be as a murderer. He loves you too much for that."

My fists spasmed, and I dug my nails deep into my palm.

"If he loves me," I managed to say, "he'll want to be the one to hear it."

The ruined priest chewed on his lower lips.

"Go to the confessional," he finally said. "If he comes, he comes."

I could barely leave the room. My legs moved on their own when I applied any weight. But I made it to the tiny wooden booths and wedged myself inside. When the door was shut, I tucked my knees under my chin and tried to quell the twitching.

Later, I don't know how much later, the window rasped open, and the foul odor of dead teeth wafted through the gap, mixed with the musk he used as perfume on important occasions.

"Aragon?" he said. At the sound of my name, for the first time in weeks, I felt warm.

"It's me. I'm sorry it's been so long."

"Has it?" he asked. His voice was moony.

"Three years, at least," I said.

"Oh. I'm sorry, I don't remember very well. Where did you go?"

"To Wales, like we always talked about. It was beautiful. I wish you could have–" I choked. I couldn't finish.

"Wales to see the Breton King," the old man said, and I had to laugh because his tone was suddenly and jarringly just like it had been ages ago. "You'll go there someday and be a knight with King Arthur, just like the ones in your books."

"I'll meet a lady," I said, "and win her heart through deeds of great renown."

He laughed, and the sound of it broke my heart. His shallow breath could only rattle, a dried leaf blowing across the stone floor. There was so little of him left here, and soon there wouldn't even be that. We had that in common, I guess.

"I need to confess," I told him.

"Then do it."

I gagged on the tears at the back of my throat, and I knew from the way his voice faltered that it shocked him.

"Jesus God and his ever-living ghost … son, what did you do?"

After a moment, I could start.

"I coveted," I told him. "I stole. I lied and lusted. I worshiped false idols. I killed."

"Hmm. A busy day for a boy as young as you."

I blew my nose on my sleeve. I wasn't sure what to say.

"He's young," the old man continued, "but just you wait and see. He'll learn to read those books, and then he'll be the greatest doctor in the world." I sniffled.

"What if he doesn't?" I said. "What if he's always just the son of a whore and an ancient priest?"

"Fool's talk," he said. "You'll remember me telling you this when the continent knows his name."

"If he can keep it," I whispered. Maybe I only thought it. He went on without stopping for the interruption.

"I'll tell you a secret," he said. "I bought those books with money I stole from the tithes."

The simple surprise of it sat me up.

"I didn't know that," I said.

"Well, I figured a doctor will do more good than a few more loaves of bread. He's going to be a doctor someday. Someday, thanks to these books. A good one."

"I won't be," I said, and kicked against the confessional against my will. "I never will." I pounded my fists into the meat of my thighs until I thought my bones would break and wished to every god I'd ever believed in for my legs to just stop shaking.

The priest's voice floated through the dark again.

"Aragon?" He asked. His hand poked through the window. I stifled a sob again and took it in mine.

"I'm here."

"When did you come in?"

"Sorry," I said. "It's too late."

"Oh," he said. "It's fine. Just make sure you wake up on time to work the kitchen."

I rubbed the back of his hand with my thumb. A noise was building on the street. It was mingled shouts, and the crackle of flames kept momentarily tame on thick torches.

"Are people forgiven who don't deserve it?" I asked in a small voice.

"Hmm? Why, what'd you do?"

"A lot of things," I whispered. I hated every memory I ever had. I hated the filth on the hem of my coat. I hated that I couldn't stop kicking with the toe that already didn't have a nail. I hated that the moment I stopped, I had to face what was waiting for me outside the cathedral doors.

Father Aragon squeezed my fingers.

"Here's what I think. There's trying to find forgiveness, and there's trying to make good."

My head hurt too much to puzzle anything else out.

"All right," I said. "I need to go."

"No." He yanked my hand to his side of the booth and held it in both of his. "Not until you understand what I mean. I'm saying forget God. He's a bastard. If he wanted you to die blameless he wouldn't have made it so easy to sin. So don't waste your life crying about it. Use the gifts I gave you for something good before you spend eternity paying for them."

Then there was a crash as he fell into the hard wood of the divider. I bolted out my side and found him twisted on the floor. I tried to hold him in an angle that didn't distort his spiderweb-thin frame too horribly, and finally he settled cradled on my lap like a little child. I couldn't even pretend to hide my sobs anymore. He took my head in his hands and pulled me into his shoulder.

"I haven't heard you cry like that since your mother died," he whispered.

"I came back to make good," I said into his shirt. "I wanted to make her proud. But instead, I did things she'd never forgive."

"Don't be stupid," Father Aragon said. "She didn't care if you're a good person." I clenched the fabric of his nightgown between my teeth and screamed as hard as I could.

"Neither do I, really," he said. "Whatever else you are, you're my son. We are of one piece. You can never be unknown because I know your name. It's mine."

He stroked my hair until dawn, telling me the things I would never hear again.

◇

I knew it was time when Vauqelin started shouting my name through the windows. Father Aragon had drifted off an hour before, so I carried him out of the confessional door and into the chapel. He didn't feel any heavier than the stack of books I'd left mired on Bentham Street. His eyes fluttered briefly when I laid him on a pew.

"Tell your mother to come visit," he mumbled. "I miss her. Just don't tell God."

I took off my coat and rolled it up for him to use as a pillow. "That was three years ago," he said. "I missed you."

"Is it a sin to miss her?" I asked and tucked the bundle below his head.

"Only when I do it," he said, so quietly I almost couldn't hear, and then he was asleep. I kissed his cheek and stretched.

Three Lips was behind me, holding a toothpick in the notch of his mouth and a hunk of bread in one hand. He gave it to me, and I devoured it in three bites. I couldn't remember being so hungry.

"Are you the one who's been taking care of him?" I asked through a mouthful.

He shrugged. "Who else?"

"Thanks," I said, and set to work straightening my clothes. Vauqelin was screaming like a holy war out there.

Father Aragon started shaking. Three Lips took his own coat off and tucked it around him as a blanket.

"He talks about you every day," Three Lips said. "I'm glad you came back while he was here to see you." He went to a window, breathed the morning air in with closed eyes, and scanned whatever lay outside. "Are you going to ask me to sneak you out a back door?"

"No," I said, and he nodded.

"Thank you. You deserve what's coming to you."

"Agreed," I said.

There's only so much laundry you can do in a sanctuary, but I did my best. I beat the soles of my boots together to thin the flakes of mud and clotted blood and pulled the loose strings out of the sleeves of my shirt. I found a bowl of water and dipped my face in it before realizing what it was. I spluttered up, horrified, to see Three Lips raising his eyebrows.

"Well," I said, "what's one more, I guess." I tried to drip as much of the holy water back into its basin as I could, and for the first time, I saw the disfigured priest laugh.

I was running out of things to do more quickly than I'd hoped. The doors gaped at me, the light of a new day outlining them in gold lettering.

"What is coming to me, exactly?" I asked. Three Lips picked at something in his molars and thought about it.

"Vitus swore yesterday he'd blot your name out of every record in town. Seems a bit dramatic, but he's got the money and thinks you'll take it personally. Everybody else just wants to kill you for making them look like idiots."

"You did all look like idiots," I said, and laughed at my own joke with a sincerity that surprised me. Everything else aside, this morning I was alive, every inch of me, inside and out.

Three Lips snorted through his nose.

"I do deserve it," I said. "Especially from Vauqelin. He was so lonely."

"Who?" Three Lips said.

"No one," I said, and sighed. "I'm almost ready. Do you have any more bread?"

I used the half loaf to make a little shrine under my sleeping father for any faeries that wanted to lend him a hand. I crossed myself for him, and then him for me, just in case. Then I apologized to Dionysus, because I didn't think I'd have time to make this one up.

The morning was cool. The birds my father loved made their music through the window, and it made me want to dance.

"Welp," I said, and Three Lips nodded goodbye over folded arms.

I opened the doors, and the mob overwhelmed me. Vauqelin floated above them on the back of his horse. I couldn't hear him over the tumult my appearance caused, but I saw his lips.

"Get the false doctor," he was screaming.

"But I am a doctor," I said back. "A good one."

The Spider Whisperer:
A Tale of Plague Dances, Peacock Spiders and Pumpkin

Deborah Henley

In 2022 it started with a toe tap, followed by a twerk. Dr. Venomer, a sixty-year-old scientist, found a new species of spider. She celebrated with a hiking boot stomp. Or so her colleagues thought...

Venomer, with her crumpled khaki trousers, emu-egg green top, wide brim akubra and magnificent magnifying glass, had discovered another species of *Maratus*, or peacock spider in the

Australian bush. The hairy creature's two big front eyes focused on the scientist. The other six eyes sat like a band around its spherical head, looking for an escape. Bright splotches covered its whole bushy body, including its peacock feather shaped buttock. When happy, the bottom could pop up and shake. The spider's bottom stayed firmly down, but the scientist's own began to jiggle.

Weeks later as she continued to frisk and flaunt like the spiders, amongst collapsing fits of exhaustion, a new team sent by the Australian Security Intelligence Organization, scoured the discovery site. They stampeded through the scraggly bush, leaving no eucalypt leaf unturned. Sheila McDonald unearthed a small bag of pepper, Turkish delights, a goose feather fan and a diary.

◇

15th July 1518 (Strasbourg)

Today my old babysitter– Frau Troffea took to the streets dancing. Astounding! I didn't think a woman built like a wagon could move with such grace. The leg kicks, finger flicks and robust arm waves. It is with moves like that, she won her husband's heart. I am jealous! Of the killer dance moves, not of the husband. Her blonde hair flying freely, her twirling skirt revealing what only her husband should see. She came across so spirited and defiant, stomping on the slate cobblestones. Frolicking around the town square despite her husband, Herr Troffea pleading with her to stop.

Herr Troffea showed up here next, demanding a refund as the cloves his wife purchased from Father yesterday came with a bonus spider. I followed his wife's lead and waved dismissively as I told him, "No." I just wished I danced as beautifully as her.

My lean frame should allow for unrestricted frivolity, but I'm Miss Two-left-feet Lacyann. Wearing my emerald necklace to compliment my green eyes, and distract from my plain mousey brown mop. And if I wear my hair half up, I can cover the collection of freckles and moles on the lower left of my neck. Oddly, if joined, they would create a spider. I should catch the gentlemen's attention. And I do so want to marry! Yet at the disastrous local dances, I always end up tripping over, out of time and utterly embarrassed. Even the peasants do not want to dance with me.

I can't wait to listen to the hearsay about Frau Troffea. While the town gossip is never as good as my father's merchant stories, it's better than nothing.

Father arrived home yesterday with cloves, cinnamon, silk and pepper to sell. He had bloodshot eyes with dark crescents under them. The brown cloak sagged on his shoulders. Lowering the hood, his thinning hair clung to his scalp, with more age spots showing. Father barely grunted during supper and then had a lie down. I have yet to see his mischievous smile. Today he headed out to begin selling his wares before I made it out of bed.

I look forward to his travel stories in the coming days and will lap up the gossip in the interim.

Lacyann

17th July 1518 (Strasbourg)

Frau Troffea hasn't died, but after days of dancing she did collapse and has been taken to a convent. The town is full of whispers asking, "Is it a blessing or a curse?"

If it gets her out of the sweeping, washing and needlework, I'm sure she'd agree it is a blessing. Others must have thought so too, as a few more have taken to the streets dancing. Though they don't smile in enjoyment, rather their faces contort.

My father, the scoundrel, is amongst them.

The group jumps here and jiggles there. I can't help but think they've all gone hopping mad!

Lacyann

1st August 1518 (Strasbourg)

Much to my disappointment, even during a dancing plague, my toes won't tap, and I've no rhythm, even in my little pinky. Dance mania is spreading. While Mama keeps reminding, "You don't want the curse of dancing. I want to know what it feels like to have my body arch, bend and twist with killer moves.

Although, they are quite literally killer moves, so I shouldn't joke as I do. Today there was our first death from dancing exhaustion. Poor Wolfgang. We have a town meeting tomorrow. In the meantime, I have been charitably skewing sausages on sticks, and waving them in front of the afflicted. I've decided to call it folk dance fishing.

Father collapsed after a particularly exhilarating night. He has been bed ridden, with only minor shakes since. Mama and I are bringing him chicken broth soup. I hope he makes a full recovery, so he can answer ALL my questions.

Lacyann

2nd August 1518 (Strasbourg)

The guild has decided we should encourage the frenzy, they're still unsure if it is from God or the devil. Bands are to be set up over the town. The unafflicted are to encourage and dance with the, "blessed." They'll even pay us for it! I've got my eye on the fair Roland. His rosy cheeks are in bloom as he moves constantly. Roland would never ask me to dance, he's a bit out of my class, but perhaps a plague will bring us together.

Raspy Father pleads for me to stay home. He wastes his small amount of breath on *that*, instead of giving me the swinging specifics.

Lacyann

3rd August 1518 (Strasbourg)

Roland may have fair features, but his dancing and onion breath leaves A LOT to be desired. My ample lips and eyelash flutters were ready to woo! Roland's uncared for hair swished as he kept stomping on my poor feet. Instead of his dreamy eyes twinkling at me, he screamed and looked like a rabbit caught in a snare. I could not tell if the scream was aimed at me, or the spider he nearly stepped on.

AND now I've got to go and harvest the pumpkins. Too many peasants are caught in dance-ageddon, so I'm off to the fields. Me, a merchant's daughter collecting piddly peasant pumpkins. At least no one has mentioned fertilizer yet.

Due to this extra workload, I have barely heard from Father. Father ONLY travels to the port and takes goods from there, but he often collects stories from further afield of fantastic beasts and enchanting architecture. He has also told me his predictions for the latest craze, T. Apparently it is a drink popular in the Far East.

Lacyann

15th August 1518 (Strasbourg)

The guild had another meeting. As the dancing spreads, it is known as a curse. Whispers in the village called me blessed. Me! Because while many of those who danced with the inflicted have now broken out in feverous frolics, I continue to move like a sack of pumpkins.

The musicians who haven't started busting a move, have moved back into their houses. All music is banned! Well, except stringed instruments. It is feared something as pugnacious as tambourines may awaken more dancing.

As many tremble in fear, the church is calling for donations to finish the cathedral. They wonder if our sluggishness towards renovating the church has brought the wrath of God. The village gave an outpouring of coins, wheat and even a horse. Throwing in money and stallions won't build the cathedral. I think God would have the sense to bring a building plague not a dancing one, if that is the cause, but Father Lovegrove insists, *God moves in mysterious ways.*

Lacyann

29th August 1518 (Strasbourg)

The dancing keeps growing. Hundreds are now inflicted. The bans on music have not worked. It has stolen the joy from weddings, this surely is the trial of the ages.

I noticed a spider family, including hatchlings in the town square today. At least something is getting on with its life.

Lacyann

5th September 1518 (Strasbourg)

Father is recovering. Unfortunately, the dancing has shaken, stirred and danced his jovial nature out of him. No good stories to report. He just tells me to *stay away from the plague, blah, blah plague is bad, blah and a little more blah*

Lacyann

10th September 1518 (Strasbourg)

Everyone is so busy dealing with this plague, most of the village doesn't seem to notice we've started to have a plague of spiders in town too. Only Roland shrieks at the little critters. Everyone else skips, dances or runs on by. Who knows, maybe the spiders want to join the dance party?

Speaking of onion-breath boy, I've been tasked with catching him. The guild has suggested we tie the inflicted up. Once bound, we are to place red shoes on their feet. Father has gone travelling to stock the town. The bound captives will be taken to the priest at the shrine of Saint Vitus, the patron saint of dance.

I'm not sure why we are heading to the saint of dance instead of the saint of standing still, but who am I to question the guild.

At least the plague is good for my fathers' business.

Lacyann

20th September 1518 (Strasbourg)

Father returned remarkably quickly. Yesterday we caught all those we could. Father helped me capture Roland. We smelt his blue-cheese feet long before we saw him. Roland mouthed *thank you* amongst his pants. After sniffing the overwhelming stench of a man who has danced for a month, profusely sweating with no wash, I knew I never wanted to marry. Which is good because it looks like I won't get the chance to anyway.

The priest, a budding sleuth, has traced the origins of the dancing plague to my father and the increasing spider population. Apparently, the eight-legged stowaways hid in father's cloves. Frau Troffea was the first to purchase this spice. He believes when the spiders feel threatened, they cause their predator to dance.

With divine inspiration, Father Lovegrove drove the plague back into the spiders. He splashed holy water and waved the preserved bottom of the saint of dance. Lovegrove blessed each dancer in attendance with the unusual relic. With a drop of holy water, a small shimmering sphere left each of the humans afflicted. The glowing ball shrunk and zapped the half a dozen spiders collected.

The spiders giveth, and with the priests help, the spiders taketh away.

Doused in holy water for protection, the priest suggested we stomp on the little critters. Frau Troffea wanted them burnt at the stake. She had toothpicks ready to tie them to.

Their spidery front legs vibrate knowingly.

"We must take them away," I called.

Beautiful splotches of indigo, cherry and golden yellow sitting on eight twitchy, hairy legs. One flicked his arms up and started to shake them, while his head nodded to a nonexistent beat. His buttock bent up, like a single round feather. It's enchanting watching the creatures move. Perhaps they are a blessing from God.

So many questions were asked. But we couldn't just kill them, for all we knew, that could release the plague again.

I have been called spider whisperer around town since. Father and I have been tasked with taking the spiders to the farthest point on Earth. My father refuses to carry the little critters, it is my task and mine alone. Even with the box blessed by the bottom relic, he fears frolicking again. As we embark to the other side of the world, the crazy flat earther Filipe, has suggested I literally drop the box off the edge of the Earth. We'll see how that works out.

Lacyann

30th October 1518 (on the road to Istanbul- not Constantinople)

Today we listened to clattering hooves approaching. Horsemen thrashing their poor beasts. Father and I moved to the side as the *clip-clop, CLIP-CLOP, CLIP-CLOP* thundered closer. Bandits! The leader had bruise-blue eyes and smirking lips. The fools asked to have everything we carried. Father tried to warn them, but a teenager slapped him.

The grubby slapper grabbed at the box I held close. As he pulled open the latch, I screamed, but one spider was on his hand. The teenager's quivering fingers dropped the box. The spiders, in a trance, lifted their front legs and began shaking. The robber's arms swung up, mouth dropped wide and bottom swayed. The baby-faced bandit was friskier than frolicking lambs.

"Oi carol kid, stop merry making," laughed the bandits. Their sniggering faces turned ghastly as the slapper, his forehead perspiring, continued to skip.

The leader, his face like a pumpkin and no neck, screamed, "Are you a witch?"

My dry mouth couldn't manage an answer.

Mr. No-neck rushed to clamber onto his stead; others followed. The slapper followed with leg kicks.

I collected the spiders. No exhilarating shake, or even hopeful hop overtook my body. We walked on.

Lacyann

30th October 1518 (Istanbul not Constantinople)

Istanbul is big, beautiful and mind blowing. I wish we could stay and explore. Father suggested we sell the spiders at the markets. However, word of our quest has spread. On arrival the locals threw food and supplies at us. Amongst the flat bread to the thigh and salad to the head, they asked us to take the curse and leave. My eyes are still burning from cumin to the face.

As we collected their throwaways, I heard mutterings that the griffins will probably eat us.

Chewing on the most delightful pink cube gift of sweet jelly goodness, Father and I stared at the Hagia Sophia longingly. With its color scheme of blue on top, creams and hints of pastel pinks underneath, it looked ready to float away into the sky. The curious building soars, with a gigantic, noble central dome top, and surrounding smaller domes and pillars. Rows and rows of rectangular windows at the bottom, and arch way windows at the top, all teasing us by not allowing us to see inside. It looked big enough to swing a pumpkin inside. Perhaps if we survive the griffins, one day we'll be spiderless and able to return.

We're following a group of caravans through the Golden Mountains, also known as griffin territory. Father and I must keep our distance, in case they fear the spiders too.

Lacyann

1ˢᵗ **November 1518 (Istanbul not Constantinople)**

Earlier today, an elderly lady came up to us. Sorrowful eyes, a button nose, pursed lips and one hobbling hip. She asked to see the spiders. As one danced, she pinched the bridge of her nose and asked, "Were the inflicted happy? Could the shaking and rhythm bring joy?"

Father told her it only brought chest pains and muscle burning.

Lacyann

2nd November 1518 (Istanbul not Constantinople)

The lady found us again on the outskirts of Istanbul, begging to try the plague. It was before sunrise, and as a light sleeper, her movement caused me to stir. Father was asleep, so I listened to her alone. Her husband had passed away. She said she was like the griffins, one mate for life. She begged with furrowed lips, "Please let me try the dance, I'll do anything to find happiness again, even if it kills me."

The creases covering her face were etched with grief, her widened eyes pleading in my silent response. But I couldn't. Would God blame me for her death? Eventually I stumbled into the darkness; thankful she was too old to follow. Yet as I ran, I wondered if I had made the right decision.

I still think of the dancing bandit, if he dies will it be on my hands?

By the time I had returned the caravans were gone.

Lacyann

6th November 1518 (Not lost, but close to it, on the Golden Mountain Trail)

I am hoping for no griffin sightings, but with each passing day our chances increase.

Griffins have the body of a lion and the wings and head of an eagle. And they're huge. Father has been told that griffin sightings are rare these days.

Good.

I think I'd rather marry a piddly pumpkin peasant, then go through the griffin territory of the Golden Mountains. Unfortunately, we don't have a choice. Soon we'll be passing the griffin lair. Apparently, there is one pair left in the mountains, maybe they'll be on pilgrimage.

Lacyann

15ᵗʰ November 1518 (Road through Golden Mountains)

I'm currently hiding. As father and I wandered on the track, I could hear a purr of thunder, followed by an ear piercing shrill. Turning toward the noise, a gust swept my face. A griffin!

Trembling, I leapt to the left as the beast tried to grab father and me. My father yelled, "I love you," as talons pierced his shoulder, lifting him away. Griffins have big bird feet at the front! I rolled down the hill. Scraping, catching thorns, tasting dead leaves. When I thudded into a tree, I didn't move. Couldn't. My heart was pounding, but my body was as still and lifeless as a pumpkin.

Should I rescue Father? But how?

Tingles returned to my limbs, but my heart won't be still.

Griffins have beaks that glimmer of death, claws to carve out innards, bone breaking bodies and smarmy eyes.

How will I even leave the mountains alive, let alone with my father?

Lacyann

STILL 15th November 1518 (Road through Golden Mountains)

I knew I was either going to die in the bush or die by griffin. I had to try and see Father, even if it was the last time!

I climbed, clenching my teeth with each branch scratch. It's like even the foliage was out to get me. Finally at the road again, I began trekking.

A purring rumbled closer and closer.

Tightly gripping the spiders, I braced for the griffin.

My arms ached, each bruise and scrape searing. But my skin wasn't pierced any further. The griffin landed, dropping me onto a pile of stiff coins, brooches and gold goblets. Father jumped up with a sharp stick in one hand.

The griffin's eagle head hissed; her mouth ready to attack us.

I opened the spider latch and threw one into her beak. The head twitched, she menacingly grinned.

The griffin's whole body went stiff, before her wings lifted out and manically in. Her head nodded as if tambourines swung. The giant drumsticks kicking, propelling her body in a bowlegged manner forward. Eyes bulged as she danced over the edge of the mountain.

Thud.

Father and I shoved gold into our rucksacks and began running. We skidded and slid over treasure as we moved down the mountain, eventually sheltering in a cave. Right now, I can barely see to write this with the glow of embers in our cavern. A shrill wail resounds through the mountains. While griffins may be killers, they're also fiercely loyal lovers…I hope we didn't just kill the last female. Father believes nature always rebounds, but that thought brings little comfort as I hear the lover cry.

I feel guilty wondering why I am the only creature these spiders won't infect, won't mesmerize? All I want is to dance, even if it is forced, and they won't give me that pleasure.

Lacyann

30th November 1518 (GREATEST WALL EVER!)

We've made it past a giant barrier. It stretched from one side of our line of view to the other. The grey bricks stood at the very least three times my father's height, snaking over the landscape. Was it built to keep the griffins out?

News of us slaying a griffin spread quickly. I don't know who saw it, but whoever did has a bigger mouth than me! Crowds have gathered, fingers grabbing, scrapping desperate people clutched at me. They ask if I am a prophet. Me? They think I am blessed.

Despite carrying our gold-filled bags, we didn't need to spend any treasure. So many followers wanted to give us things, I received the most beautiful fan made from goose feathers. The feathers are storm-cloud grey and white at the top. The food here is superb! Rice, noodles, fresh vegetables and duck, but my favourite are the dumplings! Far better than our land oysters! We need to trade dumplings back in Strasbourg instead of smarmy snails! Father keeps trying to pay, but the locals won't allow it.

I've also tried T. Most delightful. I think T drinking will be the next craze in the west and beyond. When I feel nervous about our upcoming journey, I drink the T and whisper to myself, *stay calm and carry on.* I think the mantra could really catch on.

Lacyann

1st December 1518 (Lanzhou)

We are quite far from home, but this land is too populous to release the spiders. We are in Zhong Guo, which means middle kingdom. The locals believe they're in the middle between heaven and earth. I don't know how God and the saints would feel if we sailed to them, returning the eight-legged gifts.

However, we have heard of a land south. A devout follower has offered us his boat. His great, great, grandfather, Zheng He, visited this south land. Our supporter hopes to follow his maps. He has a boat called a junk. I was a bit nervous about the name *junk,* but the boat seems to have a steady hull with three large sails that look like open fans.

We may be on our final part of the journey soon. I now have so many stories to tell, but who will listen?

Father constantly talks of Mama. I've suggested he return home and tell her all the things we've seen. I cannot imagine how mother is coping without us. She needs Father more than I do. The people here are kind, and they literally worship me. If I ever need it, the spiders will protect me.

As they call me *Spider Whisperer* here too, I've decided to always have my freckles and moles resembling a spider on display. The soothsayers believe it is a good sign.

Lacyann

10th December 1518 (Shanghai)

The spiders have required everything from me, yet they give so little back.

The ship is ready. I will sail with a crew tomorrow, but without Father. He continues to lose hair and accumulate age spots.

I want to remember him, his greying beard and round face with flat cheeks. The speckled white top of his head that sits like a giant egg, in a thin nest made of his remaining hair. Emerald eyes, much like my own, surrounded by etchings of laughter at his own jokes, curiosity from listening to other trader' stories and tears from cutting onions. The mischievous smile, with dimples on the sides, will light up when he sees Mama. He finally has his own stories to tell. I hope he survives the journey home so he can pass them on.

A soothsayer consulted an oracle bone asking, "If Lacyann sacrifices three pumpkins, will she find a land to release the spiders?" The soothsayer believes the cracks from the ancestors say yes. So, I'm off to roast some pumpkin before we sail!

Lacyann

25th December 1518 (Out to sea, in the middle of nowhere)

On a day when new life is usually celebrated, I cringe at what has emerged. While I rested, suddenly the ship's rocking went from gentle to storm like. I sent out silent prayers for the weather, to no avail. As I emerged on deck, pumpkins rolled and the feng shui was ruined. The crew on deck were inflicted, bodies ducking, diving and weaving around the ship. I counted my little friends; all were in the box. But then I realized, tiny, baby spiders glided around the deck. Once I had caught the cheeky rascals, I realized most of the crew could no longer help man the ship.

My skin will surely tan as I man the boat, yet even still the spiders won't let me join the inflicted. All my years indoors, covering myself in egg whites, wasted.

Lacyann

Mid-February (Somewhere near land)

We are close to the southern land. We see the rocks, an ember orange, and bright baby-teeth white, covered in the scraggliest trees on the horizon. I am sick of folk-dance fishing, though most of the crew dance on due to my food fishing skills.

Lacyann

I no longer know the date, nor does it matter (The Great Southern Land)

Today, I released the spiders. Joy and relief welled, growing like a magic pumpkin seed. Sending out runners and tendrils until an overflowing vine of laughter overtook my whole body. It caused my bottom to bounce, my toes to tap and the tips of fingers spread up and out. I danced as if no one was watching, because only my eight-legged friends were. My cheeks still ache from smiling. Yet I can dance and be still as I choose, so I don't have the dancing plague, but whatever I have received, it is a blessing.

Lacyann

◇

Sheila McDonald closed the diary. She knew enough, so she handed it onto her superiors. And with that, under some scraggly looking trees the Australian Security Intelligence Organization had solved three mysteries. They knew the cause and disappearance of the dancing plague in Strasbourg. The ASIO had discovered the origins of the peacock spider in Australia. And finally, they now understood why in the local Aussie pub at 3am, a dance plague regularly breaks loose. And being the ASIO they took away all evidence, including poor Dr. Venomer.

Interdisciplinary

Elizabeth Guilt

Training Course Schedule

Day 1

Session 1: Role of the lateral geniculate nucleus in the human visual pathway

Coffee

Session 2: Function of the Disruption Suit

Lunch

Session 3: Movement for minimising magnocellular detection

Day 2
Session 1: Movement for minimising magnocellular detection
Coffee
Session 2: Movement for minimising magnocellular detection (practical)
Lunch
Session 3: Stable 2-pole Quantum links (theory)

Day 3
Session 1: Configuring the Stable 2-pole Quantum Link
Coffee
Session 2: Movement for minimising magnocellular detection (practical)
Lunch
Session 3: Configuring the Stable 2-pole Quantum Link (consolidation)

I could have predicted Peter would draw up a formal schedule even though I am literally the only person taking the training. And he stuck to it rigidly, of course – I'm surprised he even permitted cups of tea in the morning breaks.

The first session was actually surprisingly interesting, all about how our brains work to help us see. Broadly, your eyes pick out a few key details, then your brain enhances the image – CSI-style – and fills in the blanks for you.

The suit that Peter's team has designed takes advantage of that. There's some basic colour-sampling and switching to help you blend in with your background, and then there's some stuff I didn't quite follow which disrupts the brain's processing. It's not like people can't see you when you're wearing the suit – but so long as you don't draw attention to yourself, they simply won't notice you're there.

As for "movement for minimising detection", let me sum up: stand still as much as possible. If you have to move, do it slowly. That's it. That is literally it. If Peter had more of a sense of humour, I'd have thought he was winding me up with days 2 and 3. He must have known perfectly well that I wouldn't be able to follow the quantum theory – and all those configuration drills! Honestly, the instructions are a little complex, but they're not exactly rocket science. As I'd have thought he would know perfectly well.

I don't need to understand all of the theory: put the suit on, twiddle the knobs correctly, pop out in sixteenth-century Strasbourg.

Excerpt from the Daily Record, May 4th

Next week, one of Mary Evangeli's top history profs will walk down a wormhole and emerge in Strasbourg...in 1518! "The physics boffins have set everything up for me," he said, clearly beside himself with excitement. "I just have to wear the suit to make sure no one spots me, or I could end up burned as a witch!"

◇

From: Prof. Malcolm Hendry <malcolm.hendry@history.mea.ac.uk>
To: Lawrence O <lawrence.oliver@cs.mea.ac.uk>
Subject: RE: great project idea!

Dear Lawrence,

Thank you for your email about using AI to process the audio captured in 1518-Strasbourg and develop a theory of language evolution.

However, the project does not meet the guidelines for the Compulsory Second-year Extra-curricular Module. Before interdisciplinary projects can be undertaken, you must complete at least one module in a subject wholly unrelated to computer science.

I believe Prof. Lavaliere may have vacancies in some medical courses, which you may wish to consider.

Regards,
Prof. Hendry

◇

And I consider it an act of great restraint that I did not end that mail with "I understand that you're regarded as some sort of wunderkind by the Cybersecurity Team, but that cuts no ice with me - you're not special, and the rules do still apply to you". Did the little squit think I wouldn't know he'd approached Helena with an equally computer-focused suggestion disguised as a music project? And then had the cheek to start lecturing her about "engagement" and the importance of "developing our students' interests". We're here to teach them, not to indulge their every whim!

Why can't today's students just knuckle down and study the way we did?

From: Professor Peter Vastarian
<peter.vastarian@physics.mea.ac.uk>
To: Prof. Malcolm Hendry
<malcolm.hendry@history.mea.ac.uk>
Subject: Very disappointed

I am extremely disappointed to read in the Daily Record that you described the Stable 2-pole Quantum Link as "a wormhole". I thought I had made clear that the S2pQL is not based on the Einstein field equations, and as such is quite different from a wormhole. It is vital that we use correct terminology in our engagement with the public.

Peter

From: Prof. Malcolm Hendry
<malcolm.hendry@history.mea.ac.uk>
To: Professor Peter Vastarian
<peter.vastarian@physics.mea.ac.uk>
Subject: RE: Very disappointed

Of course I didn't say anything of the sort. Imagine suggesting that there was any great risk of a witch-burning in that area of the Holy Roman Empire at that time!

Honestly, sometimes I wonder if physicists have any sense at all. Peter must know what ghastly hacks the Rec's staff are. Besides, no one uses the word "boffin" in cold blood unless they're writing tabloid headlines.

I must admit, though, that I am rather looking forward to it. The first historian in the world to undertake serious fieldwork in the past! The opportunity to see and hear people going about their daily lives more than five centuries ago! I think I am permitted a little excitement in the circumstances!

◇

From: Prof. Malcolm Hendry
<malcolm.hendry@history.mea.ac.uk>
To: Lawrence O <lawrence.oliver@cs.mea.ac.uk>
Subject: RE: great project idea!

Lawrence,

Even today, computers are not the be-all and end-all. It is rather presumptuous to assume I need "help" from an undergraduate with no background in history.

The rules for second-year projects have already been explained to you multiple times, and I do not appreciate your repeated attempts to circumvent them.

Regards,
Prof. Hendry

◇

From: Lee Edwards
<lee.edwards@history.mea.ac.uk>
To: Dr. Annabel Windsor
<annabel.windsor@history.mea.ac.uk>
Subject: dinner tonight?

And thank god Hendry's off to Strasbourg tomorrow, I can't bear hearing about it any more. Why on earth did the funding board pick 16thC. Strasbourg anyway?

◇

From: Dr. Annabel Windsor
<annabel.windsor@history.mea.ac.uk>

To: Lee Edwards <lee.edwards@history.mea.ac.uk>
Subject: RE: dinner tonight?

Because nothing happened. It's such a fucking boring time period that if Hendry fucks the whole thing up completely no one will notice or care.
Your place or mine?

◇

What a day! This is exactly the kind of rich detail of life's diurnal pattern which historians have always lacked. To be able to observe micro-interactions, behaviour patterns, tiny details of dress and nuances of language – this is the "real deal", as they say. No more relying on offhand comments from diarists. This will revolutionize the entire field of history. I have so much to write up – I have the full audio/video capture from the ten hours I spent in 1518-Strasbourg today, but obviously one can't rely on electronic records.
I am exhausted, but can't wait to travel back tomorrow.

◇

From: Yvonne Lavaliere
<yvonne.lavaliere@medicine.mea.ac.uk>
To: Prof. Malcolm Hendry
<malcolm.hendry@history.mea.ac.uk>
Subject: RE: bloody lawrence (pardon my French)

Hey,

NO worries about Lawrence, he signed up for one of the anatomy courses for his Compulsory Extra-curricular. He chose developmental bioelectricity.

I always start with a recreation of Galvani's famous frog experiment – it's not very educational, but it's quite theatrical and grabs their attention!

Yvonne

From: Prof. Malcolm Hendry
<malcolm.hendry@history.mea.ac.uk>
To: Yvonne Lavaliere
<yvonne.lavaliere@medicine.mea.ac.uk>
Subject: RE: bloody lawrence (pardon my French)

You have the patience of a saint! I wonder when these students are going to realise that we hate these Comps even more than they do, haha! I'm surprised they still let you have the frog in this day and age.

Best,

Malc

From: Yvonne Lavaliere
<yvonne.lavaliere@medicine.mea.ac.uk>
To: Prof. Malcolm Hendry
<malcolm.hendry@history.mea.ac.uk>

Subject: RE: bloody lawrence (pardon my French)

It's not a real frog! It's synth muscle shaped to look and respond like frog legs. Someone still fainted though – there's always one!

◇

I have now spent many days in 1518-Strasbourg, and am still overwhelmed by it each time I enter. So much detail, such fascination in the tiny moments of ordinary life. How could we have ever known that the local boys used "fence-teeth" as an insult – a reference to a particularly hated priest?

I am not unaware that many deem it a "boring" topic for the first field research project, and indeed the unlikelihood of it capturing public imagination was one of the key reasons for its selection by the Board. We could not countenance anything that would risk unhinged individuals taking it upon themselves to break in and attempt to change history. The "Kill Hitler" crowd simply refuse to understand that assassinating the man would not alter today's history books in the way they expect.

At the same time, the utmost care must be taken to disturb nothing, change nothing. Besides being basic good practice for any form of historical research, Peter and his team just do not know enough to understand what the long-term consequences might be. I'm aware some of my colleagues are extremely jealous of this opportunity, but the Board knew they had to choose someone whom they could trust absolutely!

◇

From: Malcolm Hendry
<malcolm.hendry@history.mea.ac.uk>
To: Dr. Sarah Walken <swalken@swithins.ox.ac.uk>
CC: Dr. Annabel Windsor
<annabel.windsor@history.mea.ac.uk>
Subject: RE: Symposium

Dear Dr Walken,

Thank you for your kind invitation, I would be delighted to come and speak to your faculty on November 7th.

The Strasbourg Project at Mary Evangeli's has opened up so many avenues to explore, and we are already planning research several years ahead with just the material collected this summer. You mentioned a particular interest in interdisciplinary projects; I am considering harnessing the power of AI to analyse and model language use, based on the extensive recordings I have made. The opportunities for collaboration are really quite endless! Please see attached draft outlines of my proposed research.

Regards,
Malcolm Hendry

From: Dr. Annabel Windsor
<annabel.windsor@history.mea.ac.uk>
To: Lee Edwards <lee.edwards@history.mea.ac.uk>
Subject: FWD: RE: Symposium

Oh so now Hendry puts me on CC on his external mail just to make sure I understand how fucking clever and in demand he is.

That AI analysis doesn't sound like him at all, whose idea was that?

From: Lawrence O <lawrence.oliver@cs.mea.ac.uk>
To: Dr. Annabel Windsor
<annabel.windsor@history.mea.ac.uk>
Subject: project ideas

Dear Dr Windsor,

Lee said you might like to hear some of the ideas I have around language analysis and modelling. I pitched them to Prof Hendry, but he wasn't interested.

I've attached the outlines I sent to him, but I'd love to talk through them if you want.

--lawrence

From: Prof. Malcolm Hendry
<malcolm.hendry@history.mea.ac.uk>
To: Professor Helena Smythe
<helena.smith2@music.mea.ac.uk>
Subject: RE: FWD: wanna see a photo of my d***

Helena,

I am so sorry! Of course – as you guessed – that email was not sent by me, even if it appeared to originate from my account. I have no idea how this could have happened and will report it immediately.

Apologies again,
Malcolm

◇

From: IT Security <it-security@admin.mea.ac.uk>
To: Prof. Malcolm Hendry
<malcolm.hendry@history.mea.ac.uk>
Subject: RE: fake mails

The mails appear to have been sent legitimately from your account. If they were not sent by you, it is likely that someone else has learned your password.

Please see the department guidelines on setting a secure password. Your password was flagged as not secure and has been displaying a warning on the log-in screen for some weeks.

We also recommend that you re-enable the multi-factor authentication which you disabled shortly after it was rolled out. This ensures that only someone in possession of your phone can sign into your account and was designed to prevent exactly this sort of attack.

◇

From: IT Security <it-security@admin.mea.ac.uk>
To: Prof. Malcolm Hendry
<malcolm.hendry@history.mea.ac.uk>
Subject: RE: fake mails

I'm sorry that you find the security arrangements inconvenient.

However, as you have discovered: without them, any enterprising CS student with time on their hands can cause considerable embarrassment.

◇

Why do we even have an IT Security department if the kids from CS can run rings around them like that? Security can't do their job properly, and somehow it's my fault!

I'm not sure why a student would target me, though. What on earth could they possibly learn by reading my email?

◇

From: Lee Edwards
<lee.edwards@history.mea.ac.uk>
To: Dr. Annabel Windsor
<annabel.windsor@history.mea.ac.uk>
Subject: RE:

Can we go back in time and murder Hendry?

From: Dr. Annabel Windsor
<annabel.windsor@history.mea.ac.uk>
To: Lee Edwards <lee.edwards@history.mea.ac.uk>
Subject: RE:

Do not, whatever you do, mention that to him. He has a fucking forty-five minute monologue on how actions in the past do not affect the present – with frequent references to Back From The Future (no joke he really calls it that).

I don't know why Peter made such a fuss about the process for configuring the quantum link every time. There are a lot of codes to type in, and some of the dials are a little fiddly, but I have the steps printed out and stuck to the wall. It's just a matter of following them in the correct order. Any idiot could

do it. All that "drilling", as he called it, was totally unnecessary.

I must admit I am occasionally a little tempted to misalign one of the dials slightly and peek into another historical window. From what Peter said, I'd be unlikely to end up in pre-Columbian South America or Shang dynasty China, but I might make it to, say, 14thC. Aachen. However, my work here is far too important to risk. I would hate to be accused of either incompetence with the configuration or straying from the approved procedures!

◇

From: IT Security <it-security@admin.mea.ac.uk>
To: Professor Peter Vastarian
<peter.vastarian@physics.mea.ac.uk>
Subject: Re. MEA card access system

Thanks for sharing your concerns. We are aware that there have been some reports of fraudulent building access using the swipe cards and are currently reviewing the system.

If you are aware of any specific incidents, or individuals involved, then please report them via the usual processes.

◇

The strangest thing happened today. I was standing near the corner of the market square – in Strasbourg, of course – and a woman came dancing along the street. At least, I suppose you would call it dancing. Her arms and legs were jerking around in the most peculiar way. Naturally, she attracted a lot of attention – some people even began clapping along. I can't say that she looked as if she were enjoying herself, she looked almost agonised. She was still dancing, mouth contorted and sweat pouring down her face, when I reached the end of my time for the day.

I think there is the makings of a fine paper in this event: the woman dancing was clearly the talk of the town today, but there is no mention of it in any records. If the chroniclers of the time could miss something like this, what a wealth of information we must be lacking!

◇

From: Yvonne Lavaliere
<yvonne.lavaliere@medicine.mea.ac.uk>
To: Prof. Malcolm Hendry
<malcolm.hendry@history.mea.ac.uk>
Subject: RE: Saturday?

Hi,

I'm afraid I'm busy on Saturday evening, though it was very kind of you to invite me.

I think you were unfair about Lawrence, by the way. He seems very engaged and working very hard on my course!

Yvonne

◇

I'll reply to Peter's email in the morning, or I fear I might write something I will regret. If he wants to review the recordings of my time in Strasbourg, he can watch every last second and see that I have not altered history by one jot or tittle. I haven't so much as caught anyone's eye while I'm there. As if I needed him to tell me that disturbing the course of history could have unknown and untold ramifications. Even if the populist idea that people would begin fading from photographs is a ridiculous misconception, we still have no idea of the damage that could be done.

If there is any "inconsistency in the flux net" then it is entirely a fundamental flaw in his design work or calculations. And as for the accusation that the security is inadequate! I oversaw the security arrangements myself. The guard even refused to let me in this morning until I trailed back to collect my ID pass! Peter must still be bitter that I refused to let "our" end of the wormhole be set up in the Physics department.

◇

From: Dr. Annabel Windsor
<annabel.windsor@history.mea.ac.uk>
To: Lee Edwards <lee.edwards@history.mea.ac.uk>
Subject:

You'll never believe this! Hendry has got Bob working on his pet project and apparently he laid it on really thick about the importance of security, no exceptions, no excuses, et fucking cetera. Hendry didn't bring his ID this morning and Bob wouldn't let him into his own wormhole!!! Haven't laughed so much in months.

◇

I am becoming concerned. Every day, more and more people seem to be dancing – if you can call it that. They are frenzied, crazed. More than once I've seen someone drop to the floor completely exhausted. On some days, the town organises musicians, and then at least the people dance in unison. At other times, it looks more like the writhings from a Hieronymus Bosch painting – really quite unpleasant. Although the perfect synchronicity is also extremely eerie, I'm not sure which is worse. There are certainly rumours in the town that people have danced themselves to death, although I still need to verify this.

I hope this isn't caused by the flux-net problems that Peter is still banging on about. If we have to shut down travel to 1518-Strasbourg then my research is going to be seriously hampered.

From: Jeff Gove <jeff.gove@admin.mea.ac.uk>
To: Yvonne Lavaliere
<yvonne.lavaliere@medicine.mea.ac.uk>
Subject: RE: [complaints form] teaching session
wasted

Dear Prof. Lavaliere,

My apologies that we were unable to supply the Galvastim® units required for your teaching session this morning. The units were ordered, arrived, and were booked into Stores by myself a fortnight ago. This is why they were still present on the system when you put in the request.

Unfortunately they appear to have gone missing from Stores. We have not lost them, and it is not a record-keeping error, someone has deliberately removed both boxes.

We have, of course, placed a new order with the supplier and will inform yourself as soon as they are here.

Best regards,
Jeff Gove

◇

From: Jeff Gove <jeff.gove@admin.mea.ac.uk>
To: Yvonne Lavaliere
<yvonne.lavaliere@medicine.mea.ac.uk>
Subject: RE: [complaints form] teaching session
wasted

Dear Prof. Lavaliere,

Yes of course we are investigating how this could have happened. It shouldn't be possible to remove something from Stores without it being logged on the system. In addition to the Galvastim® units some extremely expensive audio sensors and other electronics components have also been removed. This is being treated as Theft and has been reported to the MEA security team and to the Police.

Best regards,

Jeff Gove

Oh, shit. Today, in 1518-Strasbourg, I found something that should not have been there: a small box that is clearly modern in origin. I have never seen it before. Shit, shit, shit... I have to work out who could have got access and put a stop to it immediately. If anyone finds out about this, it could halt the project for weeks!

From: Lawrence O <lawrence.oliver@cs.mea.ac.uk>
To: Prof. Malcolm Hendry
<malcolm.hendry@history.mea.ac.uk>
Subject: project ideas

Prof. Lavaliere's developmental biology class is very interesting, thanks for suggesting it.

There's still loads of great data analysis and processing I could do with your Strasbourg recordings.

Maybe you're more willing to discuss it now that I've shown you "interdisciplinary" and now you've touted my ideas as your own?

--lawrence

◇

Oh, Jesus. Surely not? That little shit...is he behind all this? And is he actually trying to blackmail me?

◇

From: Prof. Malcolm Hendry
<malcolm.hendry@history.mea.ac.uk>
To: Yvonne Lavaliere
<yvonne.lavaliere@medicine.mea.ac.uk>
Subject: missing units

Bit of a weird one here, sorry. Could those muscle stimulation units that went missing be used on humans?

Best,

Malc

◇

From: Yvonne Lavaliere
<yvonne.lavaliere@medicine.mea.ac.uk>
To: Prof. Malcolm Hendry
<malcolm.hendry@history.mea.ac.uk>
Subject: RE: missing units

No, they weren't medical grade, they were the basic ones we use on synth. for student tutorials. They're not even that expensive, I don't know why anyone would steal them. So annoying as we're just getting into the final year practicals this week.

Yvonne

◇

From: Prof. Malcolm Hendry
<malcolm.hendry@history.mea.ac.uk>
To: Yvonne Lavaliere
<yvonne.lavaliere@medicine.mea.ac.uk>
Subject: RE: missing units

But COULD they be used on humans?

◇

From: Yvonne Lavaliere
<yvonne.lavaliere@medicine.mea.ac.uk>

To: Prof. Malcolm Hendry
<malcolm.hendry@history.mea.ac.uk>
Subject: RE: missing units

No, of course not. They'd hurt like hell going in, there are no proper control protocols, and the signalling is so coarse you'd have people twitching and staggering about like they were possessed.

◇

From: Prof. Malcolm Hendry
<malcolm.hendry@history.mea.ac.uk>
To: Yvonne Lavaliere
<yvonne.lavaliere@medicine.mea.ac.uk>
Subject: RE: missing units

How are the units controlled?

◇

From: Yvonne Lavaliere
<yvonne.lavaliere@medicine.mea.ac.uk>
To: Prof. Malcolm Hendry
<malcolm.hendry@history.mea.ac.uk>
Subject: RE: missing units

Sorry Malcolm. I'm really busy trying to reschedule all my practicals. If you really want to know, look at the course notes https://medicine.mea.ac.uk/resources/dev-bioelec/9/45_a/notes_FINAL.pdf

Extract from Developmental Bioelectricity course notes

Section 7 - Final Assignment

The Galvastim units are pre-programmed with a range of different signalling patterns. Each pattern sends a different electrical stimulus to the muscle, causing it to react in the ways outlined in Section 4. By carefully co-ordinating the patterns (see Section 5), the muscle contractions work together to produce fluid movement.

You will be provided with a structure built from a plastic armature (representing bones) and synthetic muscle. You will need to draw up a full schematic indicating the placement of the Galvastim units, and the sequence of patterns to be used to produce the desired movement. If you would like an extra section of synth muscle to practise pushing the Galvastim units into place, you can request one.

Please note marks are not awarded for movement, unless the supporting design work indicates that you understand why the electrical impulses from the Galvastim units are causing it!

Structures available are:

(i) elbow - this mimics a human elbow and has a limited range of movement. The highest grade available if selecting the elbow is a B.

(ii) eye + eyebrow - this is a simplistic rendering of a section of the eye area of a human face. You can implement frowns, surprise, blinking and even eye rolling!

(iii) alien wrist - this is a fun one! It is a wrist-like structure that permits movement in all planes and some rotation.

I don't see how he could possibly have got to 1518-Strasbourg. And I don't understand how you'd make those student units work together to make everyone dance in time. And I can't imagine why he's so determined to undermine the work I care about the most. But I know Lawrence Oliver is behind this somehow.

From: Nat Chatterjee
<nat.chatterjee@engineering.ac.uk>
To: Prof. Malcolm Hendry
<malcolm.hendry@history.mea.ac.uk>
Subject: RE: CONFIDENTIAL!

Hi Malcolm,

Sorry it's taken me a while to get back to you. This little device really is quite something. The construction is a bit of a mess, but the design is absolute genius.

Its function is fairly obvious: the audio sensors pick up music and it generates an electrical signal to beam out again. The clever bit is in all the code running on the chip - the algorithm for detecting "music" rather than any other rhythmic audio is amazing. The code for generating a coherent signal that looks like a pattern but is non-repeating is really smart, too.

I know you wanted to keep this quiet, but honestly this could be one of the most exciting things this department's seen in years. Who made it???

N

◇

From: Nat Chatterjee
<nat.chatterjee@engineering.ac.uk>
To: Prof. Malcolm Hendry
<malcolm.hendry@history.mea.ac.uk>
Subject: RE: CONFIDENTIAL!

PS Forgot to say - the weird thing is that it's working using radio waves, like old-skool FM! Why on earth someone would do that is a bit of a mystery, it's not like there isn't wi-fi infrastructure basically everywhere these days!

N

From: Prof. Malcolm Hendry
<malcolm.hendry@history.mea.ac.uk>
To: Professor Peter Vastarian
<peter.vastarian@physics.mea.ac.uk>
Subject: RE: possible intruder

There already were multiple "layers of security". In order to reach the room in which the disruption suit is stored, the intruder would have to swipe into the building, pass the security guard, and undo the combination lock on the storage cupboard. To reach the quantum link, he would then have to pass the security guard again and negotiate the security protocol you yourself designed for the link configuration. The security guard is the only possible weak link in the chain. One of them must have agreed to turn a blind eye.

It is ridiculous to suggest that someone would bypass the suit altogether and visit 1518-Strasbourg without it. It would be far too risky, both to themselves and to the historical context.

From: Jools Olewau
<jools.olewau@physics.mea.co.uk>
To: Professor Peter Vastarian
<peter.vastarian@physics.mea.ac.uk>
Subject: RE: Secure Access Protocol

He only bloody printed it out and stuck it on the bloody wall! Right next to the access panel! Talk about leaving the keys in the car.

So yeah, the only thing stopping an intruder reaching Strasbourg was having the right permissions on an MEA swipe card and we know there are people in CS who can spoof that with their eyes closed.

$\diamond$

From: Jools Olewau
<jools.olewau@physics.mea.co.uk>
To: Professor Peter Vastarian
<peter.vastarian@physics.mea.ac.uk>
Subject: RE: Secure Access Protocol

I've just checked the S2pQL logs - looks like the auto-monitoring had been switched off, I need to have serious words with Charlie about that.

Our intruder always went in between 1am - 5am. I guess a medieval city would be dark/asleep then? Not much need for a disruption suit.

◇

Excerpt from a letter received by Malcolm Hendry

I am writing to tell you that Mary Evangeli Academy is considering dismissing you. This is with regard to the following circumstances:

i.   Deliberate subversion of the secure access protocol for the Quantum Link, and disclosure of the secret access keys.

ii.   Failure to report obvious breaches of Quantum Link security, such as finding modern-day electronics in a historical context.

iii.   Emailing of indecent pictures to multiple female colleagues and students.

iv.   Accusations of plagiarism.

v.   Physical assault of a student, Lawrence Oliver.

You are invited to attend a disciplinary meeting on July 7th at 9 am which is to be held in the Principal's office where this will be discussed.

Searching for the
Perfect Beat

Allison Thurman

The sun sank behind the hills as Margrit and Lis ascended, carrying the laptop and controller. "Why here, Margrit?" Lis asked, breath straining with every step.

"Because it's perfect. You know that! Every single party we've gone to—"

"But we've never thrown one!" Lis huffed.

"That's why it has to be *here*." Margrit wasn't taking chances. Something about this little clearing on a hill near St. Vitus' grotto was just *special*. Even now she could feel that euphoria sparking down her spine like electricity. Tapping her toes, she started hooking up her laptop to the speakers.

◇

Avoye first heard the perfect beat in the town square.

The sound vibrated through the ground as though a carriage had passed by, but there wasn't a horse in Strasbourg well-fed enough to pound its hooves so hard. No drummers or other musicians either—between the heat and the hunger, no one had the energy to pluck a lute string.

"Stop idling." Leis glared at her, all squinting eyes and jutting jaw. He'd always been gruff, but ever since...well, they didn't speak of it.

"Can't you hear it?" she asked.

"Oh, them?" Leis jerked his chin towards the dust stirring on the square's edge. "The dancing plague. Ignore them."

Of course, Avoye had heard of the dancing plague. The latest in a string of illnesses that had burnt its way through Strasbourg, she'd heard the tales of the afflicted dancing until they died twitching on the ground in agony. But the dozen or so men and women leaping and swaying, oblivious to the jeers of the gathering crowd, didn't seem to be in any pain. They wore dirty clothes and dripped sweat, but joy lit their faces like a new dawn. "How is this an illness?"

she whispered, tapping her feet to the insistent rhythm. "They look so happy!"

"Layabouts just avoiding work," Leis scoffed.

"But can't you hear it?" How could he not feel the pulsing in the ground, in the air, in the very heart? Avoye had not felt so light and happy since she was a child. She let her basket slip from her fingers. One ill-shod foot after another, she walked, then ran towards the dancers, fighting her way through the gathering onlookers. The dancers regarded her with smiles. When had anyone in Strasbourg last smiled? When had she? A woman extended her thin arm in invitation.

As soon as she locked hands with the dancers she fairly cried with relief. They weren't mad. They'd found a secret, *the* secret. The dance was like seeing color in a gray, dull world for the first time.

"Avoye, get back here!" Leis cried. "By God, it is of the devil!"

Oh no. No, it was not. This was heaven.

The dance never stopped, and they moved as one. When one stumbled, the others would hold them up. They shared what food they could dig out of the dead, dry earth. When one collapsed in exhaustion, the others guarded them, dancing in a ring around their shaking, sleeping bodies.

Though her feet bled and the ground had worn her skirts to threads, Avoye had never felt safer. Not as a child, or as a wife, or even in the privacy of confession. So, it should not have surprised her when it slipped out.

"My son died of the pox." Avoye huffed out the words mid-spin.

An older woman in the circle squeezed her hand. Frau Troffea, if Avoye remembered correctly. She'd started the dance, darting into the street despite the summer heat and her husband's pleas. "I'm so sorry," she whispered.

"But it's my fault," Avoye said. "I never told my priest that."

"How could you have killed him?" Frau Troffea asked.

"I should have closed the windows. I should have got a physick—"

"What pox ever heeded closed doors?" Frau Troffea's hand tightened in hers. "No physick ever had a remedy. What could you have done?"

"But...*he* thinks it's my fault!" Leis never said so, but he didn't have to. Their marriage had never been warm, but he wouldn't even look at her ever since they buried Mattheus. Leis only spoke to her to scold her for crying or to cut her off whenever she tried to talk about their son. It was as if he wanted to pretend little Mattheus had never existed and would tolerate no reminders that he had.

Avoye fell to her knees, choking on her sobs. Her fellow dancers embraced her, wiping her tears and helping her lie down. Confessions whispered through the crowd. Loss, neglect, cruelty—all had received or given these and more. Sinners and victims all; only God could judge them. But simply speaking their ordeals aloud and being heard cleansed them more than the holiest water. And to think, had it not been for the rhythm, they'd never have found each other.

Yes, she ached with exhaustion, but the endless dance was better. Walking on bleeding feet was better than sleepwalking through her life, pretending all was well. Collapsing in exhaustion in the middle of the road was better than another night in bed next to Leis, staring at the wall and muffling her tears in her blanket.

She woke to hands prying her off the ground. The citizens of Strasbourg had found them and dragged her and her friends away one by one, breaking their circle and shattering the sacred thrumming.

◇

Home was the same, yet not the same.

Avoye's feet were tender but no longer bleeding. Two days in her old bed had let her heal somewhat. The grass outside her door was still gray and scratchy, and the tree still had its leaves, most still green despite autumn's arrival. Leis was the same as well. He still chopped wood and fed the chickens in grim silence while she blinked in the sunlight.

"Ah, you're up. Best get back to work," he said, not sparing her a glance. "You haven't cleaned in a month."

Avoye took the broom in her hand and stared at it as though she'd never held one before. A whole month, only a month since the deep bass had rumbled through her bones. The lack of it yawned like a hole in her soul. Yet Leis expected her to return to the broom and the kitchen as though nothing had happened.

"Aren't we going to talk about it?" she asked, barely a whisper. "Don't you want to know why? What—"

"What is there to know?" Leis said, lining up another log under his ax. "You had the dancing plague. Villagers brought you home, and you got better."

Soldier on, no time to rest, no time to mourn.

Which is why that night, and many nights after, Avoye found herself in the woods, searching.

She chased every snap of broken twig or animal call, hoping to find the euphoria of rhythm and recognition she'd found with her fellow dancers. Had none managed to re-escape? Had no one else tried? Maybe the sound had vanished forever. Perhaps, like her, they'd gone back to lives of drudgery and desperation. Whenever those doubts crossed her mind, she'd sit on the ground and cry.

"You're looking for it too, aren't you?"

She jolted at the voice in the dark. A man's silhouette lingered at the edge of the woods, dark against the already starless night. Her heart raced. She should be afraid and run, but instead, she whispered. "Yes."

"Why?" The man had a sharp scent of earth and sweat and a gentle voice. "Why pursue something that exhausts your mind and body when the council calls it plague and the church condemns it as the devil's work?"

"Because I was happy there." Avoye choked up. "We toil and starve and die and can change nothing, do nothing to make it better. The dancers heard me. They let me feel. I got more joy out of the dance than anything before or since. Joy is neither a sin nor a sickness."

She heard the smile in his voice. "Go to the river. There you will find all you require."

◇

The morning sun danced on the river like sparks, and the sound rippled through the dancers like fresh water. Fewer but familiar, they greeted Avoye with smiles. The man who had run from his failing farm raised his arms to the summer sky. The woman who survived a fire hobbled on scarred legs in time to the rhythm. The girl who fled her family and the old woman who outlived hers reveled in the music only the chosen few could hear.

Avoye took their hands. The connection filled the void in her soul like sweet wine. The stranger in the woods had been right: this was everything she'd missed and more.

But they were followed.

Musicians from the village chased them down the road. "Pray, revelers!" the chief lutist shouted. "Follow our lead so you might exhaust yourselves out of this madness!" Bless them, the pipers and lutists thought their cacophony helped, but their instruments whined over the pure pulse like a swarm of angry bees. The dancers tightened their ring and fled.

Avoye ran until her shoes disintegrated. By the time the dancers raced through Strasbourg her feet were raw again, every step leaving a smear of blood on the cobblestones. They fought their way through a knot of angry villagers, dodging rocks and sticks. Why couldn't everyone leave them alone? Was it jealousy because they'd found a way to celebrate life instead of just suffering? "Leave us!" Avoye shouted. "Let us have this! We will go to the hills and trouble you no more!"

"You will do as *we* say."

A row of priests blocked the road. They stunk of sweat and wet wool and wore grim expressions.

Avoye recognized the priest's voice. "You!" she said. "Why? Why send me to my people only to stop us?"

"'Your people'?" he said with a sneer. "We thought it an illness that would burn itself out, but you set yourself apart as though you are special. It's clear you're possessed! Strasbourg has endured this evil among us long enough."

The priests fell upon Avoye and her fellow dancers like brigands. They tied their wrists and legs. She cried out as someone ripped off the remains of her shoes, replacing them with red satin slippers so tight her feet bled through them. Avoye choked back a laugh. The richest shoes she'd ever worn, and they only served to squeeze her feet until her blisters burst.

The bed of the wagon stunk of manure, and the straw scraped her sunburnt face. Bound like cordwood, none of them could even reach out to hold one another's hands. The rhythm remained, drowning out the chants of the priests. They threw holy water on the dancers, but it only served to relieve them. How could they be damned when the holy water didn't burn?

◇

The rickety slats of the wagon jumped in time with the music, and Avoye couldn't help but twitch along with it, shuddering at every bump in the road. They started uphill, and everyone fell to the back, inadvertently kicking each other with tapping feet. "Where are you taking us?" she asked, spitting hay out of her mouth.

"The shrine of St. Vitus," said the priest from the woods. "I said you would find what you require, did I not?"

"But I am not ill. Or possessed!"

"But God has surely not smiled upon you." The priest hauled Avoye out of the wagon by her wrists, wrenching her shoulder as he shoved her to the ground. "What sin did you commit to be so afflicted, I wonder?"

"I have not sinned!" She hadn't killed Mattheus. She'd done right by Leis, for all he appreciated it. Wringing what little pleasure she could from this life was no sin either.

The sunset burned hot streaks right into Avoye's eyes, pulsing blue and violet with the rhythm of the sacred sound. "Not even St. Vitus finds our dance a sin, for I hear our song even now. God, can you not hear it? Can you not feel it?"

"It's a measure of your fall from grace that you hear anything at all!" The priest shoved something sharp into her hand. Cold lead, in the shape of a crucifix. Avoye crushed it. The points cut into her palm, leaving bloody marks to match those on her feet.

The priests dumped the rest of the dancers onto the ground. Vague shapes emerged within the bright sun: scrub brush, rolling hills opening into caves crusted with mold and moss.

The priests half dragged, half walked them towards the greatest of the caves. The cave was low but too long for the sun's rays to reach. The dense fog of incense burned Avoye's eyes.

The cave vibrated, smothering all the priests' and musicians' attempts to drown it out. It rumbled like a cat's purr, only so much stronger. Avoye plastered herself against the moldy stone and closed her eyes.

"None of that, you!" The priest shoved her to her knees alongside the other bound captives, who swayed in perfect time to the pulse.

The priests started their prayers. Avoye recognized their Latin, but she'd never known what it meant. How had the church ever supposed that they could move people with words they didn't even understand? Especially when the pounding beat crushed their words to powder.

Avoye closed her eyes. The sound enveloped her. What if she could curl up inside the music like a feather bed, pull the light over herself like a heavenly blanket?

Her limbs grew sluggish from fighting to stay upright. She slumped to her side on the cave floor. She didn't fight her bonds anymore, or the grabbing hands that tried to pull her to her feet. Only light, warmth, and rhythm mattered.

Was this heaven? Maybe not theirs, but certainly hers. Every part of her melted into the warmth, the rhythm pulsing in time with her slowing heart.

◇

Blinding sparks flew from the speaker plug. Margrit jerked away from the battery pack so hard that she smacked her head on the underside of the DJ table. "What the fuck?" she shouted. "I haven't even queued anything up yet!" But the beat pounded so hard her teeth shook.

"Maybe it's a preset?" Lis shouted back. "Jesus, it's gonna blow the speakers though!"

"I don't think so?" The sound was sharp enough to split hairs, especially coming through her cheap sound system. Margrit dodged back under the table. She touched the other connections: laptop, controller, even the battery again. They weren't even hot. "It's fine," she shouted back up.

"Well, turn it down a bit. Don't want the cops showing up," Lis said.

"Who's out here to complain?" The tourists and hikers had gone for the day and the nighttime party people were already trudging up the hill, bobbing their heads to the bass unaccountably thumping out of Margrit's fire hazard of a setup.

But then, the sound never failed at this site. No matter how cheap the equipment, the cops couldn't shut it down without an electrician. You'd have thought someone was chasing behind them, restoring every connection as soon as they unplugged it. Almost like the place itself never wanted the party to end.

Good thing too, because Margrit *needed* to dance. A night of dancing kicked away a week's worth of school, work and other everyday tedium. She'd stumble home wrung out like a wet rag but purged, relieved, and fresh for another week. She mixed one track into another, dancing all along.

"You've got the dancing plague bad!" Lis laughed.

Margrit stuck out her tongue at Lis. She'd read something about some "dancing plague" back in olden times. Allegedly, priests chased the dancers to the grotto to beg St. Vitus to save their lives and souls. She didn't know about that, but she sure as hell looked forward to dancing her own feet to blisters. Already the crowd near the edges jumped up and down as one, raising their hands for the first pounding crescendo.

Shake, Rattle and Roll

David L. Updike

Everything you've heard is wrong. Let me tell you what really happened.

My name is Beatke. You've probably heard of me as "Frau Troffea," but that's my mother-in-law, not me. Yes, there was a Herr Troffea, and yes, I was married to him. But he doesn't enter into this, not in any way that matters.

Maybe you've heard that I was diseased, that I was possessed by demons, that I was a whore who brought God's vengeance upon myself and others. Or perhaps you've been told the opposite, that I was

God's own messenger, by way of St. Vitus—that through my body the Lord spoke to the people of Strasbourg.

To these things I will say only that I was healthy in body and in mind; that I was no one's whore; and that all the saints and demons I've ever encountered have been men—and some men have been both in equal measure.

This much of the story is true: I danced.

I danced like mad, and, for a time, I made others dance just as madly—to shake their limbs, rattle their bones, roll their heads, as though their very souls were struggling to escape their bodies.

I led the way, but I didn't do it alone. And once it began, the dance had a life of its own. I take no credit or responsibility for that. Whatever you may have heard, I'm a modest soul—and now an old one as well. So before I let loose my last breath and free this spirit from its earthly bounds, it's time that I set the record straight.

Hans, Pauli, Jürgen, and Ringel were my friends. The town gossips said I was their concubine, that they shared me around like a jug of wine, but I was more mother than lover to those lads. Oh, I won't lie to you, Hans and I met a few times in the fields beyond the wall, away from prying eyes, and I had an awkward grope once with Jürgen behind the stable, but you couldn't take them seriously, not really. They were boys in grown men's bodies.

I was the one who gave them their name: Die Käfer. People thought it was on account of their odd appearance—the matching leather jerkins, the hair chopped in a straight line at the eyebrows over their rosy altar-boy faces. That haircut was my creation, too, only because they had no money for a barber, and I had no patience for anything other than a bowl and a butcher's knife. But that's not where the name came from. It was due to the bug-infested quarters they shared, which crawled with Russian cockroaches. And that, in turn, was where the dance came from.

But I'm getting ahead of myself. Let me start at the beginning.

I was twenty-two when I met them, working as barmaid at the tavern on Barfüsserplatz, the square of the barefoot friars. We were directly across from the Dominican monastery, and thus the busiest and most debauched establishment in town. I was the eldest of seven, and my father, having too many mouths to feed, had married me off at sixteen to that gout-ridden lout Herr Troffea. He, in turn, had offered my services (though not my body, thankfully) to the tavern's owner, Sigfrid Wurmser, as partial payment against his drinking and gambling debts. Herr Troffea then proceeded to quaff ale and lose at cards at an even faster rate, and our debts mounted daily in Sigfrid's scrupulous ledger.

So did the days and nights stretch out before me, an endless procession of patrons shoving steins at me to be filled and drained. In my six years as a barmaid, I'd watched men and women age decades, and not a few of them die—if not of drink, then of plague, pox, consumption, or even by their own hand. In their haggard faces, I saw my own future unraveling. Herr Troffea would drink himself to death, but not soon enough, and I would grow old, bitter and sharp-tongued like my mother-in-law, Agathe. At least there wouldn't be children to add to our misery, Herr Troffea being incapacitated in that area.

Such was my state when four lads, strangers to the town, shuffled into the tavern one night in the year of our Lord 1518. It had been raining for days, and the boys looked so damp and miserable—and so comically out of place—that I took pity on them instantly. When they came up to the bar to ask after the owner, their adorable northern accents sealed the deal. I knew then that I would serve as their protector for as long as they remained in Strasbourg.

"Herr Wurmser is conducting business right now," I said to the four hopeful faces lined up in front of me. He was in the backroom, robbing my husband blind at the Karnöffel table, which amounted to the same. I felt that this gave me some license to take the situation in hand. "Is there something I can do for you?"

There was much I could do for them, and it all came spilling out at once. They had a habit of speaking in rounds, so that you had to swivel your head back and forth and piece together the story from the bits each one offered. Here's what I learned: The four of them had come down in a caravan from Hamburg, traveling minstrels on their way to Paris to seek their fortune. They'd taken a wrong turn in Frankfurt and ended up here—a tragic mistake, given the sad state our town was in, and just the sort of thing, I soon learned, that would happen to them.

They were seeking shelter and work. Just for a few days, they said. Enough time to rest their horses and earn a bit of coin for the road. I told them we had no money to give them, and they said they'd work for food and drink instead.

"What is it that you do?" I asked.

"We play," said the one called Pauli.

"Instruments," added Jürgen.

"For entertainment," said Ringel.

"And illumination," added Hans.

"So, your work is play?" I said, not without a hint of a smile.

"Aye, and we play hard," said Hans, returning the smile.

I brought them bread, cheese and weak ale and told them to do as they pleased until closing time. You'd have thought I handed over the keys to the kingdom from the way their faces lit up. They tucked into their modest supper at once, then politely asked for refills on the ale, which I gave them. I moved on to attend to other patrons, and when I returned, they were gone. I had a shameful moment in which I thought it had all been a jest to obtain a free meal, but then the door opened and in they came carrying the oddest assortment of musical instruments I'd ever seen.

One of these was a big fiddle-like device with a crank at one end. It took two people to operate the instrument, which I learned was called an organistrum. Hans and Pauli would sit side by side, with Hans turning the crank and the two of them pulling at the row of keys along the top that changed the pitch of the strings. They worked together with remarkable dexterity, often reaching across the other to grab the keys, but they also fought incessantly and sometimes even threw punches at one another. I can't say that the result was a pleasing sound exactly—it put me in mind of the noises a goose and a cow might make in unholy union.

But when you put Jürgen's melodic lute over top of it, and Ringel's insistent banging and thumping below, the effect was rather lively. And their voices blended nicely, though I couldn't understand a word of what they sang. But before any of that could begin, they had to wait for Ringel to assemble a small village of tabors, timbrels, cymbals and bells in a semicircle that he closed into a ring by pulling up a milking stool. When he played them, it was with both hands and feet, not to mention a big smile.

That first night did not go well. Beyond the occasional hurdy gurdy player or outburst of drunken song from the patrons, we didn't have much music to speak of, and when the four strangers launched into their first song, the room divided at once into two camps—those who nodded and tapped their feet, and those who cursed and shook their fists. A few hurled chicken bones at the stage or at one another. Two young Dominican friars, who'd been quietly sitting at the back tapping their feet beneath the table, rose and headed for the door, brown robes trailing behind them. I saw what they had—the stirrings of a brawl—and wondered if I'd made a huge mistake. Would the lads be able to use those clunky instruments to defend themselves should the need arise?

I never found out, because Herr Wurmser emerged from the backroom shouting and waving his arms in the air, and not in a joyous way. After threatening the boys with a variety of crippling injuries — to both cheers and groans from the crowd — he ordered them out of his tavern. Heads lowered, they packed up their instruments. More chicken bones and not a few fistfuls of porridge followed them as they filed out the door and into the damp and dark.

Herr Wurmser, unused to such physical exertion, motioned for a chair and sat down heavily. When he had caught his breath enough to upbraid me for my hand in the affair, it was in between fits of violent coughing, which considerably dulled the edge of his harangue. Finally, depleted as an empty bladder pipe, he dismissed me with a feeble wave.

"Go," he said. "You've done enough harm for one night."

I could scarcely believe my luck. I hung up my apron and hurried out the door before Herr Wurmser could reconsider, and before Herr Troffea—who had stood by watching all this unfold with a look of bewilderment—could intervene to stop his wife from leaving.

It didn't take long to catch up with the lads. They were loading their instruments into the back of a caravan around the corner, while two bony horses stamped their feet in the rain. A chill wind prowled the streets, and I wondered if we were in for another vengeful hailstorm like those that had destroyed our crops in recent years.

"I'm sorry about what happened back there," I said, emerging from the shadows into the light of a single lamp suspended from a hook on the back of the caravan. They stopped loading and came over to greet me.

"Wasn't your fault," said the one called Pauli.

"You fed us," said Jürgen.

"And gave us ale," said Ringel.

"You didn't even get to finish your song," I said.

Hans shrugged. "We've had shorter engagements." His voice had a nasally quality, probably due to the pair of gold-rimmed spectacles he kept perched on the end of his long, hawklike nose.

"Why do you wear those?" I asked, pointing. "Aren't they for books?" I'd seen them on a few of the Dominicans, who produced them when they made a show of reading in the tavern.

"In my case," said Hans, "they're to keep me from walking into walls."

"Before he had them, he once courted a cow," said Pauli.

"You're one to talk," said Hans. "Remember when you chatted up that statue of the Virgin in Magdeburg?"

"She was standing right in front of me," said Pauli. "I suppose I was a bit soused that night."

"A bit?" said Jürgen.

"Furthest he's ever gotten with a lady," added Ringel.

This set off a squabble, during which they reverted to some northern dialect I only barely understood. I don't suppose they found my Alsatian any friendlier. Meanwhile, the rain was beating down even harder.

"Where will you go?" I interrupted.

They looked at one another, then at the ground.

"We thought we'd camp just outside the wall," said Jürgen. "We don't want any trouble."

"It's not safe," I said. Dogs and thieves prowled the night, looking for vulnerable strangers. I was determined to see that no harm came to these four.

"What choice do we have?" said Pauli. "We already asked at the monastery. The Dominicans don't want us, even for a night."

"Too busy shining their Kreuzers," said Jürgen.

"And each other's Schwänze," said Hans.

"Take care, Hans," said Pauli. "Remember München."

"What happened in München?" I asked.

"We survived," said Hans. "That's what matters."

"Barely," muttered Ringel.

"Well, I'm glad you did," I said, then felt myself flush.

"You're very kind," said Jürgen. "What's your name?"

"Beatke," I said. "But you can call me Beate."

"Beate, why did you come out here after us?"

"I was dismissed."

"So, in addition to getting ourselves tossed out," said Pauli, "we've cost this young lady her position."

"He'll have me back tomorrow," I said. "He needs me."

"You still haven't said why you followed us," said Jürgen.

"I know a place that's warm and dry," I said. "You can stay the night there, and your horses will have shelter, too." Horses left out at night had a way of disappearing in our town.

"Beatke!" came a voice from the darkness. "Beatke?" It was my husband, looking for me.

"Untie those horses," I said. "We need to go quickly."

I led them to the stable behind the old Schultz estate, which I knew to be empty. Unlike most Strasbourgeois, the Schultzes had the means to leave and had fled the previous fall, after the failed harvest promised yet another winter of misery. The town guard kept a watch on the house, but the stable out back was shielded from view. It had stalls for the horses, and space to pull the caravan inside. There was straw enough to make for comfortable, if not luxurious, bedding for the night.

Once I had them settled in, and they'd performed a round of heartfelt thanks, I left with a promise to return in the morning.

◇

Return I did, not just that day, but the next and the next. I'd sneak out in the early morning, while Herr Troffea was sleeping off last night's drunk, carrying whatever bits of food I could pilfer bundled inside my coat. Later, at the tavern, I'd draw a pitcher or two of ale to bring by at the end of the night, along with table scraps I'd deposited in a bowl hidden under the bar. It wasn't much, but they were grateful all the same. They were used to hardship. We all were, in those days.

Every day, destitute souls—sometimes a hundred or more—flocked to the gates of our town seeking food, shelter, the possibility of work. For three years in a row, much of the harvest had been lost to floods, hail and searing drought. It was always too cold or too hot, too wet or too dry. Once the Church had received its hefty share of the grain, we were left to squabble over the rest. And still the people kept arriving.

These minstrels I'd adopted were four more such poor wanderers. So why did I care about them, when so many were suffering? If you'd met the boys back then, you might have understood. There was something about them that drew me. Behind their travel-weary faces, below the profanity, the impiety, the easy mockery of all that others held sacred (or at least pretended to), there lurked an essential *goodness*, a belief that life ought to bring joy and generosity rather than suffering and denial.

It didn't hurt that they were handsome, each in his own peculiar way.

As the days stretched into weeks, I took bigger and bigger risks to keep them safe and fed. It was only a matter of time before Herr Troffea would miss me, or Herr Wurmser his food and ale, and when I snuck out to the stable it was always with an eye over my shoulder to see if I was being followed. But those stolen minutes and hours I spent with the boys from Hamburg are among the happiest I've known, filled with music and laughter.

We'd sit on blankets laid out on the floor, and they would play their old songs or make up new ones.

There seemed to be no end to their repertoire, and I often couldn't tell if they were playing a song for the first time or the hundredth. As I listened, I came to understand the words, until I could have sung along with many of the tunes. I have a fine voice, when I care to use it, but I was never asked to join in, nor was I offered any of their many instruments—not even a tambourine, which even a child could play. Although they were always gracious and kind, I can't help thinking that they saw me as a kind of servant-maid, there to cater to their needs, not to participate. That all changed with the dance.

The dance was my contribution, and it began in a jest. The stable, without its owners to look after it, had become infested with vermin. The rats and mice kept to themselves, at least when everyone was awake, but the cockroaches were growing bolder by the day. One morning I was sweeping out a pile of straw in the corner when I disturbed a nest, sending insects scurrying in every direction. I lifted my skirt and began stomping on them as they spread out across the floor. What I needed was help; what I got was a song. Ringel picked up the nearest drum and started to pound out a beat. The others grabbed instruments and joined in, and soon they had a lively tune going. Faster and faster they went, and I along with them, until the bugs were dead and the soles of my feet were covered in a disgusting brown paste that oozed between my toes. And then we kept right on going until we all collapsed on the floor, exhausted and laughing.

After that, they wanted me to do my bug dance, my Kakerlakentanz, every time I came around. I was happy to oblige. I liked being at the center of the music, rather than standing to the side and listening. Most of all, it was *fun*. I had never felt such freedom as I did when the boys were thumping and strumming, and I was stomping my way across the room. My family had never been important enough to get invited to the caroles at the finer houses, nor poor enough to join in the circle dances of the peasants. My father, the stern tradesman, wouldn't have approved of either—nor would Herr Troffea, if only because it would have required him to get off his arse. So when I danced, it was without any notion of what I ought to be doing. There was no partner to lead me, no steps to follow. I just moved as the music asked, or rather *demanded*, of me.

Pauli had made up some words to go with the tune:

Schöne Beatke, Käferstampfer,
auf ihren Köpfen tanzen
Barfuß Beatke, Käferstampfer,
tanzen sie zu Töten

Lovely Beatke, beetle stomper,

dance upon their heads
Barefoot Beatke, beetle stomper,
dance until they're dead

And so I did.

◇

It was my idea to take Die Kakerlakentanz out into the street. The boys had tried their hand at busking around town a few times, attracting some curiosity, some abuse, and very little money. They were feeling discouraged.

"What if we brought them something new?" I said. "Something they could join in?" We'd all seen the dances that broke out in the beggars' camps along the city walls. Men, women, and children, dressed in rags, thin as laths, would join hands and move in a circle, faster and faster, until the children's feet left the ground as though they were flying. Even amid the filth and dust and smoke of the encampments, everyone looked happy when they were dancing. We townsfolk had no such custom, but I had felt some of that joy in my own small way and wanted to share it.

I had also grown weary of waiting on men. My whole life had been spent in serving their needs. Bringing my father his supper, laundering my brothers' clothes, cooking my husband's midday meal, fetching steins of ale and bowls of porridge for the drunken patrons at the tavern, who rewarded my service by pinching my thighs, patting my bottom, pulling at the strings of my apron. The lads from Hamburg were a better sort of man than most I'd known, and yet I had easily slipped into the role of servant and keeper, bringing their meals, cleaning up after them. The only time I felt like I owned my body was when I gave myself over to the dance.

When I presented my idea to the group, they resisted at first.

"We can't put you out there," said Pauli.

"Why not?"

"It wouldn't be right for a lady," said Jürgen.

"And a married one, at that," added Hans.

"Since when has that mattered to you?" I said, causing Hans to flush redder than a rooster's crown.

"It would attract too much attention," said Pauli.

"Isn't that the idea?" I asked.

"The wrong kind of attention," said Hans.

"I think you're jealous," I said. "I think you're afraid that I'll steal the attention away from you."

"I'm afraid that your husband would kick you out on your arse," said Hans.

"And what of it?" I said.

"Where would you go?" he asked.

"I'm here," I said, looking into Hans's eyes, which always seemed larger than they were due to the spectacles. Hans turned away, looked at the caravan, then at the door, already plotting his escape.

It was Ringel who broke the silence. "I think she's right," he said. "T'would be a novel entertainment."

◇

And so it was that on the morning of July 14 we crossed the Ill River at St. Stephen's Gate, rattled down the narrow streets of the old Jewish quarter, past the cathedral and the bishop's palace and turned into the open space of the Barfüsserplatz. Hans climbed down, tied the horses to a post and opened the doors. We unpacked the instruments and began laying them out next to the caravan. After weeks of nearly constant rain, the sun had emerged and beat down angrily upon the square, turning the mud into dry, cracked clay.

A few passersby stopped and watched idly as we set up, but most hurried toward wherever they were going. An ancient and emaciated man, hair down to his knees, stood with his feet splayed and a toothless grin across his face, as though he'd been there all his life just waiting for this moment to arrive. He was joined by some other rough-hewn characters, men who had nowhere to go, nothing to do. If this was to be our audience, we had little hope of making any coin.

"You're sure you want to do this?" asked Hans. He'd softened somewhat since the previous day and seemed to have come around to the idea that I might be part of the group in some way other than a stand-in for mother, wife and maid.

"No," I said. "Not at all. Let's get started."

It began simply enough. Hans, Pauli, and Jürgen stood in row, with Ringel a few paces behind, his back to the caravan. Above his head, we'd hung a sign scrawled in chalk on a piece of board:

DIE KÄFER
PRÄSENTIEREN
DEN KAKERLAKENTANZ

Below the words, Hans had added a crude drawing of a cockroach standing on its hind legs. For those who couldn't read—most of them, by the looks of it—he stepped forward and announced, "Wir sind die Käfer, und das ist der Kakerlakentanz!" He turned to his companions and counted: "Eins, zwei, drei, vier . . ." Ringel took up a beat much like the one he'd played that first morning, when the dance was born. He'd added flourishes to it since then, parts that rolled this way and that before returning to the center, but always underneath was the same thump-thump-thump that drove it forward.

I raised my skirt to my knees and started to dance, shyly at first, and then with more conviction. I bounced from foot to foot, avoiding the steaming piles of horse manure. I leapt and spun, always landing on the beat. Puffs of dust rose around my feet as I traced patterns in the clay, outward loops like the petals of a flower, always returning to the center. Hans, Pauli, Jürgen and Ringel went out with me on each excursion, came back with me to the center. And always the beat, thump, thump, thump.

The first to join me was the old man with long hair. I smelled him before I saw him, and when I looked up, there he was, moving up slowly, eyeballs bulging like some crazed saint. He danced circles around my circles, his head rolling atop his shoulders as though it might break free and fly away. I marveled at how a man of his advanced age and decrepitude could summon so much energy. Surely there were other forces at work upon him, though whether divine or profane I could not say. He was followed by others, and soon I found myself amid a mass of bodies, all swaying and jerking and twitching to the beat. They kept coming, and the music kept playing and the dust rose around us in a cloud that must have been visible beyond the walls.

I don't know how long we carried on. People say it was hours, and I have no reason to disbelieve them. At some point, there was a commotion at the edge of our swarm of bodies, and I saw a man pushing his way through the dancers. It was Herr Troffea, come to reclaim his wife. His face was red, his eyes wild, his mouth forming angry words I could not hear. Someone collided with him, a wild-haired woman of some forty years whose red tunic, drenched in sweat, hung loose about her shoulders. He shoved her roughly aside, and she fell sprawling across the ground. Others grabbed at his limbs, clothing, hair, stuck their fingers in his face. He shook them off and kept coming. I retreated toward the caravan, thinking to take shelter there, but then the long-haired old man appeared behind him. The old man was entirely naked now, his body spattered with dirt and blood and excrement. He sprang in the air and wrapped his arms and legs around Herr Troffea's neck and waist, riding him like a donkey or a lover. They spun round a few times before crashing to the ground, and then the others closed in.

The last I saw of my husband, he was being borne triumphantly above the heads of the jubilant dancers, like a trophy from the hunt.

◇

It was well into the evening, the setting sun casting shadows across the square, when Ringel finally broke the spell by standing up, kicking over his drums and shouting, "I've got blisters on my fingers!"

A stunned silence fell over the assembly, though many continued to move. It was an eerie thing to watch, this dance without music. Some bellowed for more, but Ringel had already climbed into the caravan and pulled the door closed behind him. When it became clear that there would be no more music that night, the revelers began to disperse, many with limbs still twitching to a tune that played on in their heads.

In the midst of the strange enchantment that had come over us, we'd forgotten to ask for money, and no one had given us any. Instead, they'd brought offerings of bread and wine, laying loaves and jugs out in a row. I must have had something to eat or drink, though I've no memory of it. All I know is that I crawled into the caravan and fell at once into a deep sleep.

I awoke nestled between Ringel and Jürgen. Even in sleep, Ringel was keeping the beat with his rhythmic snoring. I could feel the pulse of his breath against my neck, the faint thumping of his heart. As I lay there, listening intently, I imagined one great and eternal song playing in the heavens, while we here on earth caught only the merest snatches of the tune.

I pried myself free of my sleeping companions and climbed out of the caravan. The morning sun was already ablaze over the steeple of the New Church, and it promised to be even hotter than the previous day. My feet screamed with each step as I hobbled behind the caravan and crouched to make water. When I limped around to the front, I found Hans sitting on the runner, loaf in one hand, jug in the other. I sat down next to him, and he tore off a hunk of bread and handed it to me, followed by the jug.

Already, some five-and-twenty people had gathered in the square and stood watching us.

"So it begins again," said Hans.

"What happened to us?" I said. "And what are we doing?" I didn't really expect an answer.

He shrugged and nodded toward the onlookers, whose number had already grown since I'd sat down.

"It's not about us anymore," he said. "It's about them."

By the time the other three awoke, the crowd had reached at least a hundred. Many I recognized from the previous day, including the old man—who had, mercifully, availed himself of a bath and a new set of clothes—but others were new. Peasants in tunics and clogs were joined by tradesmen, pilgrims and even a few wealthy burghers in showy silk turbans and ladies in tunics of fine linen. Some, drawn by curiosity, stood to the side, arms folded across their chests, waiting to be amused. Others stood nearer and looked to us with pleading eyes, as though beseeching us to heal them of their afflictions.

Pauli, Jürgen and Ringel were still eating their breakfast when the clapping began. It was started by a white-robed young Dominican acolyte with a downy yellow beard. He was soon joined by others until nearly everyone was clapping and chanting "Kä-fer, Kä-fer, Kä-fer!" Hans rose and clapped along, arms raised in the air. A cheer erupted as the boys took their places at their instruments.

Ringel, who had ended the previous night's revels, once more took up the beat. Perhaps his blistered fingers had miraculously healed overnight, but my bruised and bloodied feet had not. It seemed impossible that I would ever take another step, let alone dance the day long. And yet when the music began, I found myself on my feet again, dancing.

◇

Of that second day, only bursts of memory remain—of faces and torsos, arms and legs; of hands clasping one another; of bodies moving in circles. One of those bodies must have been mine, but it was more like we had all joined into one body, a great segmented beast that wound its way along. This was how we kept ourselves going, the strong pulling the weak until the weak became the strong, and so on. When we finally stopped, far into the night, everyone lay on the ground right where they were and slept. It must have rained, for when we awoke, we were soaking wet. We rose and once more took up the dance.

It was on this third day that the authorities finally intervened. I don't know why they waited so long, nor why they arrived when they did. Perhaps it was panic at seeing us gaining in strength and numbers. The delegation that entered the plaza from the direction of the bishop's palace was headed by the ammeister himself, Herr Drachenfels, flanked by the rest of the town council, a bevy of priests, and even the bishop. Dozens of guards armed with halberds and shields followed in their wake, along with a group of townsmen. Among the latter I spotted Herr Wurmser, his corpulent figure further swelled with pride at being in such distinguished company.

The delegation was greeted by a chorus of jeers, but they'd already succeeded in bringing the dance to a halt. One of the councilors handed the ammeister a parchment, which he flourished and began to read, his words unintelligible beneath the taunting throng. He was still intoning when a wine jug sailed over our heads and smashed at his feet. That was all it took. Shields raised, the guards advanced on the crowd.

In the chaos that followed, I caught glimpses of the boys as they hastily loaded their instruments into the caravan, but each time I fought my way closer I was swept back by the cross currents of bodies, some fleeing from the guards, others rushing toward them brandishing improvised weapons. Instead of reaching the caravan, I found myself among a group of some twenty dancers encircled by guards and cordoned off from the rest of the crowd.

Thus trapped, I watched as Pauli, Jürgen and Ringel climbed in, and Hans closed the doors behind them. He untied the horses and catapulted himself into the driver's seat. As the caravan pulled away, Hans turned once and looked back. I'd like to think he was looking for me, looking *at* me, but who knows what he saw through those little round spectacles of his. And then he faced the road ahead, and the boys turned the corner and disappeared from my life.

◇

As for me, I left town in a different caravan. Our hands and feet bound, me and my fellow captives were bundled into the back of two ox carts. Seated across from me was the hairy old man, who had once again shed his clothes. I wondered if our destinies were now linked in some way. The guards had driven the rest of the crowd from the square, and the councilors and priests stood in a circle, conferring in hushed tones. They looked in our direction from time to time, but no one spoke to us. For all we knew, we were about to be hung in front of the bishop's palace as examples to others who might feel the urge to dance. But when the procession finally got underway, we passed through the city gates and into the countryside.

There were four carts in our caravan, each pulled by two oxen. In the lead cart was a group of priests and friars—among them, I noted, the two young Dominicans who had been at the tavern that first night when Die Käfer arrived. Bringing up the rear were the guards, who made rude and lascivious gestures at us when the priests weren't looking. We prisoners sat on the hard wooden floors of the other two carts as we bounced along a rough track past abandoned farms and towns emptied of people. After days of constant motion, our limbs now protested at their restraint. The guards unbound us only to relieve ourselves, and once to forage for fruit, most of it unripe, in an untended orchard.

On the second day, we arrived at a town tucked against the base of a ridge. High above, the towers of a fortress jutted from among the trees. Unlike others we had passed, this town was inhabited, and its denizens watched us rumble past with curiosity. The old man, who had easily slipped his bony wrists and ankles free of their bonds, struggled to his feet and stood smiling and waving at the crowd, as though this were a pageant and he was the guest of honor. This caused quite a stir among the townsfolk, until one of the guards, with the handle end of his halberd, shoved the old man backward into our laps.

Our procession halted at the cathedral, where we were met by four local priests. The guards untied us and herded us out of the cart, and then we followed the priests up a steep rocky path toward a large bluff of red sandstone. At its base was a cave around whose entrance pilgrims congregated. Atop the bluff was a small chapel, and it was here that we were led.

Inside we found a chaotic scene, as pilgrims jostled to get closer to an altar at the far end of the narrow space. Some carried live chickens that squawked and flapped their wings, filling the air with white feathers that floated upward toward the peaked ceiling. In front of the altar, the pilgrims parted to step around a woman who lay convulsing on her side, white foam gathering around her lips, as a man and two young children bent over her.

Upon the arrival of our group, the priests who had escorted us began clearing the others from the room. Young acolytes rushed in to remove the fowl and other offerings from the arms of the exiting visitors. The prone woman, still spasming, was lifted and carted away. The chapel now emptied of all but our party, we were each handed a small cross and a pair of red shoes and told to put them on. My feet were so swollen that I could only get them halfway inside the shoes. Thus attired, we shuffled toward the shrine like an army of wounded returning from battle.

The altar consisted of four carved and painted panels depicting the same robed saint. In one, he was submerged to the neck in a large cauldron; in another, he offered his hand for a lion to lick; in a third, he stood at the center of a group of dancing courtesans, resisting their vulgar advances. In the final panel, he was ascending into the clouds on a beam of light. This figure, we learned, was St. Vitus, patron of dancers, but also of those afflicted with palsies and seizures, struck by lightning, or attacked by animals. We stood, faint with heat, hunger and exhaustion, as the head priest said Mass. We were then offered communion, which was the first food or drink that had passed our lips in many hours. Several of our party fainted and were carried away by acolytes.

When the rest of us had partaken of the sacrament, the priest lifted his arms above his head and commanded: "In the holy name of St. Vitus, dance! Dance for your Lord and Savior!"

I fell to my knees instead.

I was escorted to a convent, where the nuns bathed me, dressed the wounds on my feet, clothed and fed me. Apparently, my prostration before the altar had been interpreted as an act of devotional confession, and there was even some hope that I might join their order. When I made it clear that my callings were of a secular nature, their charity ceased, and I was bundled back to Strasbourg.

Of the journey home, there is little to say except that I survived. The town to which I returned was strangely subdued, the people going about their business with tight mouths and downcast eyes. Perhaps they had always been thus, and I had just been accustomed to it, but it seemed strange to me now. As I walked along, it occurred to me that I had nowhere to go. I couldn't return to the Herrs Troffea and Wurmser, even if they would have had me. That would have been a kind of death. I couldn't return to the stable by myself, for what would be the point?

And then I heard a distant thump, thump, thump and my heart leapt. I rushed forward, following the sound. Around the corner I discovered four youths playing for a small knot of dancers. They resembled Die Käfer, right down to their leather jerkins and severe haircuts, but even from a distance I could tell it wasn't them. As I got closer, I saw that they had a wooden sign leaned against the wall behind them, like the one we had put up in the square, except that theirs read "DIE ROLLENDE STEINE." The dancers were even younger than the players—who couldn't have been more than eighteen—and their movements, though lively, seemed more intentional than those of the Barfüsserplatz dancers. I watched for a while, but they took no notice of me. To them, I was just another onlooker. As I moved on through the town, I stumbled upon several more such groups—Die Schildkröten, Die Frösche, Die Nachtvögel—each with its own little cluster of dancers. Hans had been right: Whatever this was, it no longer belonged to us. And it was catching like the plague.

◇

I left town that same day, traveling on foot at first, and then in yet another caravan—of Bohémiens, this time. They were headed not toward Paris but north into Germania. We parted in Berlin, but not before the old matriarch, who took a shine to me, had taught me to read the Tarot. I continued on to Hamburg, where I became a soothsayer, and a very good one at that.

Reports of the "Dancing Plague of Strasbourg" eventually reached even this far north, and though some included me by my old name—for now I was simply Beatke—I did not recognize myself in them, and the lads had been completely written out of the story.

I hope they made it to Paris. I hope they found their fortune, or at least made a bit of coin along the way. I always did love those accents.

As for me, I remain here in Hamburg, turning the cards until the deck runs out and I join the great eternal dance that awaits us all.

Michael Wolgemut (German, 1434–1519). *The Dance of Death*, 1493. Woodcut illustration from *Liber chronicarum* (aka *Nuremberg Chronicle*) by Hartmann Schedel. Bayerische StaatsBibliothek, Munich.

Acknowledgements

Speculation Publications has had an exciting year. The success of the *Lady in White,* released in October of 2021, coupled with the launch of the publication company has kept us busy as bees in late summer, and it's been worth every moment.

We would like to give a big thank you to Patricia Allingham Carlson for once again providing her amazing art to grace our cover. And a special thank you to LCW Allingham for her insight, drive and her understanding of complicated publishing matters. We at Spec Pub would not be here without her, and we are grateful.

Thank you to our spouses for their unending support with everything Spec Pub. And our gratitude goes out to Bill Donahue, Chris Bauer, Ef Deal, and Don Swaim for their support and encouragement. We appreciate all of you.

Speculation Publications would also like to thank all the writers who submitted to our inaugural call for submission. We received an outrageous amount of amazing stories for *The Dancing Plague* from all over the world. Talented writers creating beautiful worlds. It was difficult to whittle the selection down to only nine. But the nine that we selected were the stories we had been waiting for.

Lastly, we thank you, our faithful readers. Some of you have been with us from the beginning, in 2019, with our first release of *The Lost Colony of Roanoke*. Some are just discovering our utter speculations. Those excited and beautiful faces we see at each launch party and the support we've received on social media is what makes this work wonderful. We are honored to have you along for this exhilarating journey of creative discovery and speculation.

-River Eno

ABOUT THE AUTHORS

JD Byrne was born and raised around Charleston, West Virginia, before spending seven years in Morgantown getting degrees in history and law from West Virginia University. He's practiced law for nearly 20 years, writing briefs where he has to stick to real facts and real law. In his fiction, he gets to make up the facts, take or leave the law, and let his imagination run wild. He is the author of six novels and numerous short stories. He lives outside Charleston with his wife and the two cutest Chihuahuas you've ever seen.

Jocelyne Gregory is an MFA graduate of the University of British Columbia's School of Creative Writing and a graduate of Simon Fraser University's The Writer's Studio. She has worked as a graduate teaching assistant and a manuscript consultant with The Writer's Studio and community libraries. She has written reviews for children's books with UBC's Young Adulting Review. Her works have appeared in *50-Word Stories, Emerge16, New Zealand's Flash Fiction*, and *Zooscape* (2023). She lives on British Columbia's Sunshine Coast.

Elizabeth Guilt lives in London, UK, where history lurks alongside plate glass office buildings and stories spring out of the street names. She dances at any and every opportunity. Her fiction has appeared most recently in *Cosmic Horror Monthly, Luna Station Quarterly* and *The Colored Lens.*

Deborah Henley is a geeky hippy living in regional NSW, Australia. She enjoys laughing at life's absurdities with her history buff husband. Deborah's writing can be found in various publications including *mumlifestories.com, Mindfood magazine* and *Furious Fiction*. She is currently working on a middle grade fantasy novel.

C. Owen Loftus is a writer, teacher, and actor based in Salt Lake City. He's a graduate of the University of Utah, and is married to a strange and lovely ocean spirit. He has a background in educational, journalistic, and business writing, and is proud to release his first work of fiction with Speculation Publications. He believes in aliens, but not Bigfoot, and is on the fence about daemons.

Jennifer Lee Rossman (they/them) is a queer, disabled, and autistic author and editor from the land of carousels and Rod Serling.

Allison Thurman was raised on a diet of *Star Wars, Monty Python*, and *In Search Of* and makes a lot of things, lately out of words. Her writing has appeared on *Tall Tale TV* and in the *Washington Independent Review of Books*. She lives in the metro DC area with too many books and not enough swords and is currently working on her first novel.

David L. Updike's work has appeared or is forthcoming in *Journ-E: The Journal of Imaginative Literature*, *Hobart Magazine*, *Philadelphia Stories*, *Daily Science Fiction*, *365 Tomorrows*, and *Grimoire*. His story "Feral Wives" was a winner of the 2020 *Marguerite McGlinn Prize for Fiction*. He lives in Philadelphia, where he runs the publications program at an art museum.

Romy Tara Wenzel is a writer on Melukerdee country, Tasmania, passionate about folk horror and weird history. Her preoccupation is with liminal states: the spaces between becoming and unbecoming, wildness and refuge, inter-species communication and ecstatic transformation. Recent publications include short stories in *Dark Mountain*, *Folklore for Resistance* and *Folkloric*, and shortlistings for the *Speculate* and the *Tasmanian Writers' Prize*.

Speculation Publications

www.ingramcontent.com/pod-product-compliance
Lightning Source LLC
Chambersburg PA
CBHW070509300726
48975CB00007B/2377